Table of C

Dragon Lovers Menage Second Chance Romance

By: Lilly Wilder

Foreword

A homecoming leads to a second chance for my enemy who wants to be my lover.

Home. It has so many connotations. For me it's a place I wanted to leave far behind. After being shunned by my mate when I got pregnant I fled with my unborn child to the city, intending never to return again.

But then my Dad gets ill and I'm forced to return to take care of him. Now I have to worry about my kid meeting his father, Tristan, a man I once loved and have now grown to hate. I know that my son is going to have questions, and it's a father's job to teach our children about their dragon shifter heritage, but I'm afraid my son is going to turn out to be a bad boy just like his father.

Then there's Gordy, Tristan's best friend. He was always kind to me. He's still kind to me now. Maybe kindness is what I need.

Maybe I can reject Tristan just as he rejected me.

Dragon Lovers

Chapter One

Kira

A mist rolled around the small town. In the background purple mountains rose, blotting out the stars. My stomach churned with nerves and anger and frustration. I blinked away tears, hating that I had to come back here, somehow knowing that my life was always going to lead me home. Plumes of smoke rose from chimneys. The wide main road of the town wended like a snake. Big trucks sat motionless next to a diner. I could smell the eggs and bacon wafting towards me.

A small hand squeezed mine.

"Is this it, Mom?" Deke asked. He looked up at me with his wide eyes. I swallowed a lump in my throat every time I looked at him. He was so much like his father.

"It is. This is my home." I sighed. "And it's going to be your home too."

"But I liked our old home. Why did we have to come here?" he asked in a whiny voice. I understood his frustration. It wasn't as though I wanted to be here either. It had been five years since I left. Deke knew nothing of this place. This wasn't home to him. There were no bad memories lingering here, nothing of the past to haunt him. I had sworn that I would protect him from all this, that I would make sure he never knew of his heritage, but it was inevitable that some promises would be broken. I just had to stay strong for him.

"You know why, Deke. We won't be here for long, I promise. We'll be back home as soon as we can," I said, thinking about the bright lights of the city that glittered like stars and the safety that came in numbers. Sure, there were things that I was afraid of and parts of myself that I had to hide, but these were a small price to pay for the sake of peace of mind. And I knew that deep down Deke would never truly belong in the city, that there would come a time when he would want to know where he came from, but it was too early for that.

Still, I tried to put on a brave face and make the most of the situation.

"You get to meet your Grandpa. I'm sure he'll be happy to see you," I said.

"I don't want to meet anyone," he replied, pouting. It was late. He was tired. We both were. Hunger gnawed in my stomach as well, and I assumed the same was true of him. Dad's ranch was still a little while away. The bus had stopped short of bringing us into the town. It had already disappeared into the distance, its headlights fading into darkness. We were going to have to stop off for some food before making the final stop. Before we went in I looked up to the sky, just in case I saw the flapping of wings. I hadn't just left this place behind when I left, but I had ignored my essence as well. The people who lived in this town weren't ordinary people; we could turn into dragons. It was just another thing I had kept from Deke, and I knew the longer we stayed here the harder it would be to hide it from him.

I walked into the diner, glancing around warily. I nudged Deke into a booth and when the waitress came over she smiled and asked what I wanted. Deke had waffles, I had some bacon, eggs, and toast. The waitress smiled again and then she lingered. I cringed.

"Say, don't I know you?" she asked, chewing her gum so loud I could hear it smack between her lips.

"I don't think so," I replied through gritted teeth, keeping my head bowed and my gaze averted. I glanced at my reflection in the window and ran a hand through my black hair. When I left it had been lighter, but I had changed since then. Five years was a long time, although it wasn't long enough to forget. The waitress shrugged and called out the order. Deke leaned back, closing his eyes. I felt bad that he had been dragged along here. I would have done anything to stop him from coming back here, but I had nobody I could entrust him to. I had never learned to let anyone else take care of him.

The food came quickly. I told Deke to hurry. The longer we were out in public the more likely it was that someone was going to recognize me. I knew it was inevitable, but I wanted to delay it for as long as possible. Damn Dad for getting sick, and damn me for caring enough to come and take care of him. My hands trembled as I gripped the fork, feeling a thousand eyes staring at me. My throat ran dry and the food lost all its taste. I had tried so hard to escape, so hard to make a new life for me and Deke, but now we were back here and it all seemed so hopeless.

It had been hard enough to leave in the first place, was it going to be impossible the second time?

I tried to not let my thoughts turn to him as well, but I couldn't stop them. They pulsed behind my eyes, making my head throb. I rubbed my temples and wished I could dig my claws into my brain and tear them all out. I had done the same to my heart a long time ago.

The door to the diner swung open. Deke wasn't being cooperative, pushing his food around his plate like it was a toy.

"Eat up," I said.

Footsteps crashed against the floor. They stopped.

"Kira?!"

I cringed and looked away, but he was already coming towards me.

"Oh my God, it is you! What the hell are you doing here?" he asked. I turned to face him, rising to put myself in between him and Deke by instinct. It was a mistake. He grabbed me and pulled me in for a hug, his arms around me like a vice. His beard rubbed against my skin. The scent of Old Spice tickled my nose and the heat of his body scorched me. He stepped back and gazed at me in wonder, as though I was some ghost that had appeared.

"I can't believe it's you," he said. "After all this time... I never thought I'd see you again. Tristan is going to be over the moon."

"Hey Gordy," I said in a dry, flat tone. I threw myself back down in the seat, hating the knot in my stomach that appeared when he mentioned Tristan. Gordy's blue eyes sparkled with wonder and his lips had curled into a smile that wasn't going to leave his face any time soon.

"What are you doing back here?" he asked again, and then his gaze fell on Deke. "Is that..."

"That's Deke. My son," I said, glaring at him. There was a look of recognition in his eyes. "I'm here because Dad is sick. I came to look after him."

"Oh yeah, I heard about that. It's a tough break. I'm sure he'll be glad to see you. It's been so long."

Not long enough, I thought.

"Yeah, well, I'm just here until he gets better, and then we're going to head back to the city again."

"At least you'll be around for a while. It hasn't been the same around here without you. We've all missed you," he said, and placed a certain emphasis on the word 'all', and I knew who he meant. I couldn't believe Tristan would miss me though, not after what he had done. I pushed the painful memories down and told Deke that we had to get going.

"How are you getting to your Dad's?" Gordy asked.

"Walking," I replied.

He barked a laugh, before he realized I was serious. "Kira, you can't walk out there at this time of night. There are coyotes and all kinds of things. Let me give you a ride."

"I can take care of myself," I spat, but then I looked at Deke who was practically passed out. It had been a long ride from the city, and if I was to walk it meant I was going to have to carry him.

"Come on, let me give you a ride. It'll give us a chance to catch up."

I reluctantly nodded.

DEKE BARELY STIRRED as I buckled him into the back seat, before I got into the passenger seat beside Gordy. The engine roared and two bright beams of light slashed through the darkness. Dirt and gravel crunched under the wide tires.

"I almost didn't recognize you with that hair," he said.

"Yeah. I thought I'd change my look."

"Well, things haven't changed so much here. They're pretty much the same as when you left. Even Ol' Edith is still baking her pies, and we all thought she'd give up the ghost years ago. Tristan is going to-"

"I don't care what Tristan thinks or feels," I snapped. "You know what happened. You know why I left. Loyalty is an admirable quality Gordy, but sometimes it can blind people too."

"But the kid..." Gordy said, glancing in the rear view mirror at my sleeping child.

My heart trembled at the thought of anything interfering with mine and Deke's relationship. I tried to swallow a lump in my throat but it just wouldn't go away.

"I'm not here to see Tristan. I'm not here to see anyone. I'm just here to take care of my Dad and then I'm going to be gone again," I said, my voice as sharp as a knife.

"It doesn't have to be that way, Kira. I know a lot of crap happened, but it's all in the past."

"Not for me it isn't," I said, and glanced at Deke again. He was the only thing that mattered to me now, and I wasn't going to let anything, or anyone, hurt him. Thankfully, Gordy remained silent for the duration of the journey. Darkness stretched out all around the car, as though we were driving through an abyss. I had almost forgotten how quiet it was out here, and how impossible it was to drown out thoughts.

The soft glow of lights appeared as my father's ranch grew nearer. Gordy pulled up and leaned back.

"Thanks for the ride," I muttered. I got ready to leave, when Gordy grabbed my wrist.

"You know he's going to find out you're here, and he's going to want to talk to you," he said, his eyes glowing like sapphires even in the depth of the night.

"He can want whatever he wants, it doesn't mean I'm going to give it to him. He sealed his fate long ago," I said.

"Tristan is the kid's Dad. He deserves to meet his son."

"Deserve hasn't got anything to do with it. Do you think I deserved the way he treated me? Tristan didn't want anything to do with me or Deke then, so what makes you think anything has changed?"

I slammed the door behind me, wrenching my wrist away. It was the first time I had let a man touch me in five years. I gathered up Deke in my arms and marched towards the house, breathing with relief as Gordy reversed and drove away. Anger simmered within. How dare he try and say that Tristan deserves anything when he was the one who rejected me. He was the one who turned me away when I needed him the most. And now Gordy thinks I should just walk back into Tristan's life and give him a chance to be a father? No way. He had that chance once and he blew it. I'm not the kind of woman who gets rejected twice. All I want is to take care of my Dad as quickly as possible and then leave again, because there's nothing left for me here, and there's nothing Deke needs to learn that I can't teach him.

I rapped my knuckles on the door and waited for Dad to answer. My gaze drifted to the sky. I started to remember how good it used to feel to spread my wings and soar through the air. It had always been a good way to release some anger, but I couldn't let Deke see that yet.

Chapter Two

G ordy
      I watched Kira leave before pulling away in my truck. Damn she was a sight for sore eyes. Didn't think it was possible for her to get any hotter than what she had been before, but I guess the city was good for her. Motherhood seemed to have its charm as well. I get why she's protective of the kid, but there's no denying who his father is. Deke looks just like Tristan. It's uncanny. How does she manage it all the time, living with a reminder of the man she left behind?

I guess there's no love lost. I can't blame her after the way things ended, but now that she's back here maybe there's a chance for them to work things out. It hasn't been the same since she left, as though something has been missing from our town. As I drove away from the ranch I was in shock, stunned because I never thought I would see her again. It had always surprised me that Tristan hadn't gone after her when Kira had left. I always figured if I had a child I'd do anything I could to track them down, but Tristan and I are cut from different cloths. But she's back now, and who knows how long for? It might well be the case where she stays for a while. It's rare that any dragon ever leaves, and surely it's got to be better for the kid to be among his own kind as well. I can't imagine what it would be like for him to grow up in a city with people who would treat him as a monster if they ever discovered his true nature. I shuddered at the thought. The truck crawled over the dirt road, a crunching sound underneath the tires. It made me laugh really. Driving wasn't exactly the most efficient way to travel when I could have just spread my wings and soared through the air, but we all developed our different habits and I guess technically we are just as much human as we are dragons, although it's difficult to deny the more primal aspects of ourselves.

My stomach rumbled as I hadn't gotten anything from the diner like I had intended, and I was going to have to ignore it again because Tristan needed to know the news. Kira would probably hate me for it, but he was going to find out eventually so it might as well be from me. I had no idea how he was going to take it. We didn't talk about Kira or his son that often. It was almost as though she had disappeared from the world once she had disappeared from our lives. It was the way she wanted it. But deep down I knew it had taken a toll on Tristan. That kind of thing is bound to, I mean, they were mates and then she was pregnant and then she was gone. It was the first time that I started to see Tristan as a flawed human, no better than the rest of us.

Up until that point I had always had a kind of hero worship about him. He was the strongest of us, the best of us. There was nobody who could fly as swiftly or hunt as well as him, but then when his mate fell pregnant he rejected her. I never agreed with it, not that I had any say in the matter at all, but I've always thought that if you have a kid you should keep them around. It's just the right thing to do, but not everyone thinks the same way, and Tristan has definitely always done things his way.

I drove along the barren land, gazing out to the horizon that had been my home all my life. I hoped that Kira's anger would fade eventually so that I could ask her about the city and the outside world. It was something that I had always been curious about, and she now had the answers. I pulled up outside Tristan's ranch. The long porch was illuminated by an electric light, a trap for flies. I got out of my car and walked up it, hearing the fervent buzzes, the death throes of these flies. The lights were on inside so I knew he was home. I rapped my knuckles on the door and then opened it, walking across the creaking floorboards towards his huge lounge that connected with the kitchen. In the middle of the room was a long, wide table with a wooden backless bench beside it. Tristan was sitting there, hunched over, poring over a map.

"You got anything to eat? I'm starved," I said as I headed towards the kitchen.

"Probably something in the fridge. Didn't you go to the diner?" Tristan asked without looking up from the map.

"I did, and you'll never guess who I ran into there," I said as I reached into the fridge, pulling out a sandwich that had been wrapped in foil and a bottle of beer. I caught another one in between my fingers and dragged it out, placing it on the counter. I cracked them open and took one to Tristan.

"So look at this," he said, gesturing to the map. He seemed to have ignored what I said. "I went for a flight earlier and I think I might have found something. There are these mountains here, and I found some caves. I haven't gone exploring yet. I think it's going to take a long time and I'm going to need supplies, but I think that might be where we're going to find him."

I rolled my eyes. "Tristan, why are you putting so much effort into this? Even if Black Fang was out there he probably died generations ago. It's a story we were told as kids to frighten us."

"But I saw him," Tristan said, glaring at me. There was a crazed look in his eyes, an obsession that had been with him since childhood. "I know I did. And he's still out there somewhere. If we could just find him then we could learn his secrets and we can be immortal, just like him."

I leaned against the counter and took a huge bite of the sandwich, speaking between big chews. "Speak for yourself. I don't think I'd want to stay around here forever."

"You're crazy," Tristan said. "This is all we have. If we're not alive then we're nothing. Why wouldn't you want to be a part of that?"

I shrugged. "I just think life is special because it's going to end one day. If it just kept going on and on then eventually I'd get bored and I'm sure I'd want it all to end anyway."

Tristan shook his head as he curled his fingers around his beer and brought it to his lips, taking a long glugging sip. "Well I'll be sure to remember you after you're gone," he said. I looked at him with something akin to pity. I wasn't sure when it had happened, but he had lost himself in this delusion that Black Fang was out there waiting to be discovered. To me it was just a waste of time. I polished off the sandwich and tossed the foil into the bin, washing it down with a deep swig of beer.

"So aren't you going to ask me who was at the diner?" I said, trying to hint at the fact that something important had happened, although he had already turned to his map.

"I don't know, did someone take a wrong turning and get lost here?"

"No, actually it's a familiar face. Kira is back."

As soon as I mentioned her name he stiffened and turned slowly. "Kira?"

"Yeah, and she's not alone either. She's got the kid with her, Deke."

"Deke?" he replied, as if feeling out how the name felt on his tongue. It was the first time he had been made aware of his son's name after all. I felt a little strange that I had been the one to meet his son before him. It felt like an intrusion, but I suppose such things couldn't be helped.

I wondered what his reaction would be, and was a little disappointed in him when he scowled.

"What's she doing back here? She doesn't have a right to be here," he spat.

"She has just as much right as anyone," I said. "And she's here because her Dad is injured. She came back to take care of him."

"He can take care of himself. She should have stayed away." He rose from the bench and began pacing around the room, his steps furious with anger. "What the hell does she think she's doing coming back to my town?"

"She was born here as well," I said, trying to make him see reason, but his anger had already risen inside and threatened to spill over, pouring out of him in hot fury.

"She was born here and she made a mockery of me. She never deserved to be here and she doesn't deserve to be here now. She should never have come back. She kept my son from me."

"You told her to leave. You were the one who rejected her."

Tristan twisted his head and glared at me, staring daggers into my eyes. He walked up to me until he was inches away from my face. "You don't know anything. You weren't there. This has nothing to do with you and everything to do with her. I'm going to need to speak with her," he said.

"I don't think that would be a good idea at the moment."

"What do you mean? She was my mate, and that boy is my child."

"Well, she didn't seem that enthusiastic about seeing you is all. I'm just saying I don't think you're going to get a friendly welcome. You should probably take your time, maybe wait until she's been here for a few days before you go and see her, let her get settled in. It's been five years Tristan, she's going to need some time to settle in."

"She knows what she's getting herself into by coming back here. She can't expect me just to stand by and ignore her, not when she's got my child. I can't believe you didn't tell me this sooner, Gordy, what kind of friend are you?" he said, and promptly marched out of the house like some kind of wayward storm. I sighed and shook my head. Kira's return was going to cause a lot of problems, and I had a feeling I was going to get caught up in the middle of it. I walked across the room towards the table where I glanced at the map. The territory was covered in X's, which indicated places that Tristan had explored and turned up no clues. He had circled the area he had found recently though and had dotted it with exclamation marks. I rubbed my chin and then exhaled deeply, wondering where this was all going to lead. If Black Fang had ever existed at all then he must have died a long time ago. I don't care what the stories said, nobody was immortal, not even dragons.

Chapter Three

Tristan

    I slammed the door behind me. Dying flies buzzed as they were caught in the trap. I sniffed the air and could sense their frazzled bodies. Other than that the night was still and quiet, although Gordy had just told me that my world was turning upside down. It was clear that he had no idea how much this really meant to me. He should have been far too tactful, and how could he have let Kira come back without bringing her to me? She was the mother of my child and I needed to see him. It had been too long already.

    I pinched the bridge of my nose. She had always been emotional and rash. I needed to speak with her, but what was I supposed to say? I needed to think, to clear my head. She always made things so muddled inside. I stepped away from the ranch and arched my head back. I closed my eyes and felt the primal energy swirling inside me, the bestial essence that was my honorary gift, my blessing from the Ancient Ones, the thing that made me strong and great and better than normal humans. It burned like fire within me. It was always there, just waiting to get out, and every time I felt it, it reminded me of Black Fang's story. My flesh shuddered and cracked. The pain was immense, but it was followed by exquisite relief as it hardened into scales. My body grew, my eyes squinted and I suddenly became aware of so many other things in the world. My long tongue ran over sharp teeth. I hunched over too as a tail swung behind me. My legs were thick, my arms short yet powerful. My jade scales were dark in the night, as though an emerald had been dipped into obsidian liquid. Huge wings stretched out of my back, each one of them tapered to reveal a bony spike at the end. I beat my wings and took off, rising into the sky. The world tumbled away from me as I spun and increased my momentum, leaving it all behind before I suddenly stopped and stretched out my wings, catching an air current and holding myself in the sky, my silhouette stark against the soft glow of the moon. Then I ducked down and circled the town, trying to clear my mind, but all I could think about was the story of Black Fang, a story that been told to me again and again by my Mother when I was young.

BLACK FANG WAS ONE of the Ancient Ones, beings who were an amalgamation of the best of humanity and dragons. They could till the land and build houses, but they could also shift into terrifying creatures that ruled the skies and struck fear into the heart of anything they encountered, either beast or man. The Ancient Ones wanted to build a settlement that would be safe for their kind, where they could shift at will without having to hide their true nature from the other pure blooded humans, who saw them as sport and a thing to hunt. But not all the Ancient Ones wanted this. There was one, known now only as Black Fang, his human name lost to time, who thought that being human was only holding him back. He saw the destiny of the dragons to shed their human skin completely, leaving behind only a dragon. His scales were said to be as dark as the night itself, and his breath was so fiery that it had charred his teeth until they were black. He believed that the heart of a pure dragon was so strong it could never die, so he pursued ways to free his soul of the shackles of humanity so that he might be able to attain this immortality.

One day he left as the others did not share his ambitions. He flew off and was never heard from again, although over the years there were many sightings of a black shape in the distance, but it was never confirmed if it was Black Fang or not.

THE STORY WAS TOLD as a warning so that children would appreciate both halves of their souls. Some, like Gordy, believed that it was nothing more than a fable made up from adults who were so afraid that children would reject the human part of them and embrace the dragon. I didn't believe that though. I was sure that Black Fang had gotten what he sought and that he was just waiting for someone to find him, an equal who could prove himself as great as Black Fang.

I remember the moment I saw him as clear as day. I was young, still finding my way in the world. The act of flying used to tire me out terribly and I could not travel long distances. I looked to the distant cliffs and I saw him, this black shape in the distance. It hung there for a moment, and then it disappeared. It felt as though Black Fang was sending a signal to me, challenging me to find him. For years I had searched, despite everyone telling me that I was wrong and foolish and stupid for believing a story. I knew he was out there though. I could feel it in my blood. He and I were one and the same. We both wanted to be better than we were, to push ourselves to our limits and become more than a shifter. Nobody else understood though. Nobody, especially not Kira.

And now she was back, back with my son.

Over the last five years I have often thought about that final moment, that heated argument where our souls had crashed together and erupted in incandescent fury. There was so much to love about her, and so much to be infuriated by as well. Now she was back and of course she had to be, because she couldn't have gone an eternity without bothering with me. I suppose that was the only downside to being an immortal; having to put up with maddening people. Gordy didn't know any better either. Then again he had always had a soft spot for her and that wasn't something I was ever going to change. Perhaps now that she was back he would be able to see Kira's true nature.

But the fact that she had brought my child... the boy she had called Deke. I can't say that I particularly approved of the name. In fact,

I wonder if she had chosen it purposefully to get under my skin. However, a name does not necessarily define a person's nature. Perhaps my son would be more willing to see the truth of the world, to join me in my hunt for Black Fang.

My lipless mouth smirked as I thought of this, starting to see another possibility extending. What I really needed was help, and although the child was just a boy he could still prove invaluable. Perhaps Black Fang would reappear when he realized that he would not have just one soul joining him, but two. Of course I would have to find a way to fight against his mother's influence, but that shouldn't prove to be too much of a problem. The boy had been alone with her for five years now. I imagine that he had long grown tired of her and could use a change.

With this decided I descended to the ground again, pressing my wings flat against my body as I drilled towards the ground, feeling the wind whipping against my face and scales as I built up speed. My heart raced as the ground came hurtling towards me, only stopping the sensation when I flung my wings open abruptly, moments before I hit the ground. They caught the air like a parachute and my motion was interrupted. I flapped them a few times, hovering above the ground, before I landed and shifted back into my human form. Bones crunched and I grit my teeth to combat the pain as I returned to my human self. Whenever this happened I always felt as though I left something behind, something precious.

Before me stood Rock's ranch. The old man was like granite, and while I was sad to hear that he was ill, I wasn't there to wish him well. I was there to talk to my mate and get to the bottom of why she had returned.

It was time for a reunion that had been five years in the making.

Chapter Four

K^{ira}
My anger faded as soon as I stepped in the door and saw Dad standing there. I'd been keeping in touch over the phone for the past five years, and he had even come out to the city to see me shortly after I had moved away, but it had been a long time since I had seen him and it shocked me at just how old he looked. His shoulders were hunched and he moved slowly. It seemed as though much of his body mass had simply sloughed away, and all that was left was the barest essentials. He had a hacking cough, and it seemed like only a matter of time before those essentials were taken away as well. My heart trembled at the thought of losing him, and it was clear that this was going to be harder than I thought it was going to be.

He didn't act like he was having trouble though. He waddled towards me and gave me a hug. His long white beard was rough against my cheek.

"And this is the little tyke?" he asked, gazing in wonder at Deke. I had Deke pressed against my shoulder. He was practically fast asleep. "I guess I'm going to have to wait until tomorrow before I get to spend time with him," Rock said, his words punctuated by the cough again.

"Yeah, I'm really sorry, but it was a long journey. He's been wanting to fall asleep for hours. I'm going to put him down and then I'll be back, okay?" I said, heading upstairs to the room where I had spent so much of my life. Moonlight poured in through the window, illuminating the room in a soft silver glow. I placed Deke down in the low bed. He stirred a little as I pulled the blanket over him, not even bothering to try and get him undressed. I kissed him on the forehead and smirked as I looked around at the old posters that were still hanging up. This was a kind of time capsule of my life, back before Deke had existed. It was so strange to think of the past because he was such a big part of my life. It didn't seem right that there was a part without him in it. I was about to leave when something caught my eye. It was a photo that had been stuck between a mirror and a wall. There I was, smiling with a drunken haze in my eyes, caught between Gordy and Tristan. I remembered the night well. Back then things seemed so perfect, as though there was no doubt that everything would turn out for the best. How naïve I had been. I sighed and let the picture drop to the dresser, and then pulled the door ajar, ready to let Deke sleep.

DAD HAD FETCHED ME a beer, and had gotten one for himself as well. He was sitting in his reclining chair, and gestured for me to take a seat on the couch.

"Are you sure you should be drinking that?" I asked.

Dad scoffed and shook his head. "Ain't no doctors that are going to stop me from drinking beer. What's the point of living if you can't enjoy the finer pleasures in life? Next thing they're going to tell me is that I can't enjoy being with a woman," he said.

I raised my eyebrows, and then decided that I didn't want to know the particular details about his liaisons with the fairer sex. "Dad, I hope you are taking this seriously."

"Oh, of course I'm taking it seriously. How can I not? It's not every day you're told that your body is betraying you."

"Well, we need to fight this, okay? That's why I'm here. Whatever you need, I'll get it for you. I'm not going to leave until you've beaten this, right?"

"Or until it beats me," he said with a wistful look in his eyes. The memories I have of my Dad are that he never took things lying down. He never backed off of anything, sometimes to his detriment as he never knew how to leave a fight. But that was one of the things I loved about him. That was one of the characteristics of which I was most proud, and that I hoped Deke would inherit as well. I sidled along the couch and reached out to him, taking his hand in mine and squeezing it tightly.

"Don't talk like that, Dad. There hasn't been anything that can beat you yet. If you managed to get through losing Mom then you can get through this," I said, adding a smile that I hoped would give him some strength.

"I was a younger man then, and I had you to live for."

"You still have me, and you have Deke, too. He's excited to meet you."

"But you're not here all the time, are you," he said, turning his gaze towards me. My throat tightened. Leaving had been the right choice for me and Deke, but there were other people who had been hurt by it, like Dad. My head dropped and a few strands of hair fell across my face. I took my hand away from his and took a swig of beer.

"It wasn't all my choice you know, Dad."

"I know, but you could have stayed. You could have fought. This is your home just as much as his."

"And it would have been difficult to stay here. I had to do what was right for Deke. I'm sure you would have done the same in my position," I said, but from the look on his face I wasn't sure that he would have. I closed my eyes and inhaled deeply. The last thing I wanted was to get in an argument with him about this.

"All I want is to help you get through this, Dad. I'm sorry that life hasn't been easy. I've been trying to make it as easy as possible."

"I know you have, sweetheart," he said, and there was a moment where he looked forlorn. "I didn't mean to make you feel guilty. It's just hard when you get to my age and you realize there are fewer days ahead of you than there are behind. When you're young it all seems like it's going to last forever. Right now, I can imagine why Black Fang did what he did."

A shadow fell across my face. "Don't even mention that name to me," I said darkly.

He just took a sip of his beer and nodded. "You know what I meant though," he sighed. "Anyway, how are you coping, love? How is life in the city?"

"It's not been too bad. I have a nice job working in an office. It's simple work with good pay, and flexible hours so I get to spend time with Deke."

"And is there anyone special in your life?"

"No," I said, averting my gaze. I knew the question was coming, but it still felt as though he slipped a knife between my bones and struck right at my heart. He groaned in disappointment and dipped his head, scratching his temple.

"Kira, how many times have I told you? Life is about making connections. You have to try and find someone special. It's too long to spend it all alone. You deserve to be happy."

"I am happy, Dad."

He pursed his lips and gave me a withering smile, as though he knew that I was lying.

"It would be good for you, and for Deke. Speaking of the boy, has he...?" Dad asked, raising an inquiring eyebrow.

"Not yet. To be honest, I wouldn't mind if it takes him a lifetime. Being a dragon doesn't bring anything with it but problems."

"You don't mean that."

"I do, at least in the city. It's hard enough as it is, let alone when you're hiding something like that. I have to keep people at arm's length. I can't ever let them know. I don't particularly want that for Deke."

"Then maybe that's a sign that you should come back here permanently."

"Dad-"

"He should get a chance to be around his own people, Kira, and really, so should you."

"I can't, not after what happened," I said folding my arms across my chest.

"It's been five years. Maybe things change. Nothing stays the same forever. You should know that better than anyone."

"Maybe I should give it ten years, or twenty, or maybe Tristan is the one who should leave."

"Just because you stay doesn't mean that you have to socialize with him."

Now it was my turn to give him a withering look. "Dad, do you really think Tristan is going to leave me alone? He's not going to, not with Deke around. I don't want Deke to have anything to do with him."

"How are you going to manage that while you're here?"

I hadn't worked that part out yet. I gnawed on my lower lip and scratched behind my ear. "I'm not sure, but I'll find a way."

We spoke for a little longer. I tried to steer the conversation away from Tristan and Deke and all the things that were difficult to talk about, but there were so many things that were difficult, not in the least Dad's illness. I didn't want to act like it was his death knell, but I had to be the rational one and at least think about the possibility that he could be dying. It felt cruel to introduce Deke to his grandfather only to then tell him that said grandfather was dying, but Deke might also have thought it cruel to have been separated from his father for the first five years of his life. I had this sinking feeling that no matter what Deke was going to end up hating me at some point, and I had to brace myself for the storm that was going to come and find me.

As it happened there was another storm brewing outside the door, and this was one that I was hoping would wait until the following day at least.

Chapter Five

Tristan

The door opened and she was standing there, this woman who had been my mate, who had held my heart, the mother of my child, and the one who had been gone from my life for the past five years. I stared at her, trying to find the differences between the woman I knew and the one she had changed into. Her hair was black now. It made her features more pronounced. Our relationship had been so intense it was difficult to forget the passion that had risen between us. Even now I could still remember the fire of her fingers running down the middle of my body, or her wet lips, luscious and open, waiting for me to pluck a kiss from them. It made my heart tremble, but I had to be strong. I couldn't allow myself to be a fool for her again. She stood a few inches shorter than me, but her defiant gaze always made her seem taller. There was a scowl on her face, and I could see in her eyes that there was no love lost for me.

"I don't want to speak to you, Tristan," she said bluntly, and went to slam the door in my face. I shoved my foot in, bracing myself against the pain as the door hit the side of my boot.

"But I want to speak to you," I said.

"I don't have the energy for this. I'm too tired. If you really want to do this then we can speak tomorrow," she said, but I wasn't about to have the terms dictated to me like this.

"It's been five years, Kira. If you think I'm going to wait another moment longer then you're mistaken."

"I'm just here to look after my Dad. That's all. As far as I'm concerned we can keep out of each other's way."

"How is Rock anyway?"

"Just fine, not that you care."

"I don't think that's fair. I've been checking up on him now and then. I do like to take an interest in all the members of the thunder," I said. Some dark energy flickered in her eyes and she clenched her jaw.

"I mean it, Tristan. I'll stay away from you if you stay away from me. That's what you want, isn't it? You didn't want me around."

"Because you insulted me. All I needed was your trust, your support, and you practically laughed in my face. You wouldn't be laughing if you had joined me. Maybe with your help I would have found Black Fang already. Maybe then your father wouldn't have to be afraid of dying."

"He's not afraid of that," she snapped, "and he's not dying. If you're still obsessed with Black Fang then I guess things haven't changed much around here. I would have thought that you would have seen sense by now."

I almost went apoplectic. After all this time she was still as disrespectful as ever, and it reminded me why I had rejected her in the first place. I didn't need her distracting me.

"You don't know what you're talking about. I'm closer than ever."

"I guess it was a good thing I left then, so that you could be alone with your studies. Having a family would only have gotten in the way, wouldn't it?"

"Yes, it would have. But now you're back, and now that you mention it I'm looking forward to meeting my son," I said, trying to look past her to see if Deke was waiting beyond her. She angled her body to block my view into the room though.

"You stay away from him," she said in a low growl, narrowing her eyes. "He might be your child by blood, but you gave up all rights to him when you told me to leave."

"That's not how this works. He's my child and he will always be my child. You can't fight against nature, Kira."

"I can fight against anything I want, and if you think that you can get your dirty hands on him then you have another think coming. You stay away from him, you hear? Otherwise, I'll tear the wings from your back and make sure you can never find Black Fang." The hatred in her voice was evident and I was almost proud of her in a way, to hear this sheer hatred and the force of nature roiling inside her. It was clear to me that she hadn't lost any of what had made her special in the first place. It was just a shame that she could not see the wisdom of my words. I hated the idea that she was going to indoctrinate my son into this way of thinking. He deserved better than that, and despite what she said I vowed to find a way through to him, a way to connect with him and teach him all about the things she ignored. We had our nature and we were proud of it. Knowing her, she hadn't even told Deke that he was a dragon, if he hadn't exhibited the signs of his true nature.

Behind her Rock came into view. The old man had once been a formidable warrior, but his age had caught up with him and now he looked like a gnarled old tree stump, someone who had nothing to offer the world anymore because his strength and his vigor had all been drained away. It disgusted me to see him like this and I dreaded the idea of ending up like him. It was the worst fate I could think of, and it made my insides knot and twist.

"I think you had better be on your way. It's getting late. There's plenty of time for talk later," he said. I could have pressed the issue, but this was still his home, and I guessed that I had gotten under her skin for enough tonight.

"I'll be seeing you around, Kira. I'm sure there's plenty of time for us to catch up on everything we've missed, and whether you like it or not, our son is going to ask questions about me. He deserves to know the truth."

I turned my back and walked away from the ranch with their gazes boring into me. I felt the heat of Kira's ire on my back. It was a feeling I hadn't felt for a long time, and it felt kind of good to have her back.

It was certainly going to be interesting, and I was sure that our next conversation was going to be one for the ages.

Chapter Six

G ordy
I awoke with the dawning sun. The sky was slashed with deep, vibrant hues of orange and red, as though a painter had allowed their creativity to run away with them. The air was fresh, although dry as usual. The dark sand stretched out to the mountains and rose up, covering the huge stony growths. Light swirled before my eyes and as I gazed into the distance I thought about Tristan's aims. There were many times when I had tried to see what he claimed to have seen, but if Black Fang was still out there then he hadn't presented himself to me. I rubbed my eyes. It would have been much easier had Tristan never gotten this idea into his head, but he had been fixated on it for as long as I could remember and I had long given up trying to sway him from it. But now that Kira was back... I had no idea how he was going to react.

I got in my truck and stopped at the store before I headed to Rock's ranch, figuring that Kira could do with seeing a friendly face. I had no idea how long she was going to be in town for either, and I wanted to make the most of the time.

I pulled up outside the ranch and swung my legs out of the truck. I went onto the porch and knocked strongly on the door. It took a few moments, but Rock answered, squinting at me with his cloudy eyes.

"Bit early for you, ain't it?" he said.

"It's a bit early for you to be up as well."

"Not much point in wasting the day, especially when you don't know how many days you have left," he replied.

"I bought you some supplies. Figured you could use them now that you have a couple more mouths to feed. I thought it might save Kira a trip to the store," I said, holding up the bag of groceries so he could see. He jerked his head up and walked deeper into his home. I went into the kitchen and started unloading the groceries.

"How is she doing? Did she get a good sleep?" I asked.

"I presume so. Don't think she's too happy being back here though. Had a visit from your friend as well. I assume it was you who told him she was back," Rock said with an accusing glare.

There was a slight catch in my voice. "I had to. He's like a brother to me."

"Yes, well, it meant we had quite a rude intrusion. You have to know-" Rock stopped himself mid sentence when he realized that Kira was coming down the stairs. My gaze drifted towards her and my throat tightened when I saw her slender legs peeking out from her robe. The rest of her body followed. The robe clung to her curves and I felt a warm wave of arousal ripple through me. Her hair was wet, and a few drops still lingered on her flawless skin. She had no sense of modesty, and gave me a challenging look as she walked past me into the kitchen. The scent of lavender trailed through the air past me, and I was entranced by the sway of her hips. Tristan had always been a lucky man. Lucky, and a fool.

"Thanks for the supplies," Kira said. "Dad, would you mind giving us a moment?"

Rock looked at me, and then walked away, leaving us in peace. Kira spoke as she unpacked the rest of the bags, putting the items in various cupboards.

"So what brings you here today? Is this just something you're doing to make up for telling Tristan that I'm back?"

"You knew I was going to do it. I couldn't help it. Tristan and I-"

Kira held her hands up. "I know, you're practically brothers. I get it. I haven't been gone that long you know. But it really wasn't the kind of thing I needed on my first night back. You could have at least waited until the morning to tell him. After that trip all I wanted was one night to myself, one night where I could rest and deal with the crap with my father and think about how I'm going to possibly endure being here for... I don't know how long," she placed her hand on her forehead and looked at a loss for words.

"It's not going to be that bad, right? This is where you belong after all."

"You didn't say that at the time," she said, making me feel so small with those steely eyes of hers. "You never spoke up when Tristan told me that I should leave, when he rejected me."

"I tried to speak to him, but he wouldn't listen. I'm sorry, Kira. Maybe I should have tried. I have to admit that it has changed my perspective of him. Before that happened I didn't think he would ever do something like that. I didn't think he could be so ruthless."

"That made two of us," she said, scowling. I had never really thought about what it was like for her to be alone in a new place, having to figure things out for herself while at the same time having to take care of the baby. The more I thought about it the more Tristan seemed like the bad guy in all of this, which was so hard for me to admit when I had spent my life practically worshiping the man.

"I noticed he hasn't found Black Fang yet. I thought after all this time he might have given up on it. Has he still not realized he's been chasing after something impossible?"

I sighed. I still felt the need to defend him even though some of the things he did were indefensible. "He actually thinks he has made a breakthrough. He's been going out there regularly, exploring all the territory he can. He won't rest until he's found Black Fang."

Kira snorted. "Then he'll be waiting a long time to rest. He's going to die at some point. We all do. Black Fang is just a story. I guess he's put so much time into believing it that he can't just admit that he's wrong. What else would he do with his life? What would he do with his time? If he could just focus on Black Fang and leave the rest of us alone our lives would be so much better," she said.

"I had hoped that things would be different but... well..." I sighed, and decided that I didn't want to talk about Tristan any longer because it seemed to be a sore subject, and the last thing I wanted was to upset her. "How is your Dad doing?"

She shrugged. "He's okay. Thanks, by the way, for checking up on him. He mentioned that you've been by a few times."

"No worries. I try and keep touch with all the old timers. They're so far apart they don't get to see many people, and after what happened with Louella..."

Kira gave me a quizzical look.

"She died, but nobody discovered her for a week and a half. By the time we got there the smell was..." I curled up my face with disgust at the thought of finding her there, the smell had somehow found its way into the back of my nostrils and there were moments when I was forced to relive that horrible moment again.

"I didn't realize that. It must have been hard for you to cope with," she said.

"It was, but we get by. How has life in the city been?" I asked.

"It's been like you would imagine life in the city to be."

"How did you cope with it? You know, with being different to everyone else?"

Kira ran a hand through her hair. When she folded her arms across her body it had the effect of pushing her breasts together, creating a deep valley of cleavage. I tried my hardest to avoid looking, but I was unsuccessful. I may have been a dragon, but I was still mortal, and I still had hot red blood coursing through my veins.

"I just tried my best to fit in. I never let anyone too close though. I couldn't risk them finding out."

"So you never shifted, at all?" I asked, my mouth agog. Kira shook her head. I gasped, unable to believe that she could go five years without shifting. Five years without unleashing the beast within us, all this pent up energy with nowhere to go. No wonder she was irascible.

"No, I didn't, because I couldn't risk it. If anyone had seen I don't know what would have happened to Deke. There are always people watching in the city, Gordy. There are always cameras, and everyone is always on their phones. Even if I went high in the sky in the middle of the night I'm sure that someone would have caught it in one photo. I couldn't risk it."

"But you must be suffering so much."

She shrugged again, tilting her head to the side. "You get used to it," she said. I couldn't imagine ever getting used to it.

"Well, at least you're back here now. You can let your wings spread again."

"If I want to. I might just leave that all behind me as well."

"Kira, you're a dragon. You might have left this place, but you can't leave that part of you behind. Surely with you and Tristan as his parents it is in Deke too." I didn't mean to have my tone so accusing, but I never realized things had been this bad. Sure, she had left this life behind her, but to leave behind the dragon part of her as well? I couldn't understand it. I had to shake my head in disbelief at the two of them. Here was Kira who wanted so badly to forget about being a dragon, to tear away the parts of her soul that made her so special, and there was Tristan who wanted to get even deeper into those parts of his soul, to become a true dragon and shed the human parts. I'll never understand how they managed to get together in the first place. It seemed as though it had been doomed from the very beginning. I know it was a cliché that opposites attract, but this seemed ridiculous.

Kira swept a hand through her hair and scowled.

"People don't have to be like their parents," she spat. "If Deke does start showing signs of being a dragon then I'll tell him. But until then he doesn't need to know."

"He doesn't need..." I started, but checked my tone because I didn't want to anger her any more than I already had. "How are you going to keep it from him? You should at least prepare the kid."

"Don't tell me how to parent my child. You don't have kids. You don't know what you're talking about."

She bristled with tension and radiated heat. Aside from being a little intimidated by her (Kira had always been the type of woman to never back down from a challenge and always say what was on her mind) I still pitied her. She had been through so much, and there had been a time when we were good friends. Her being back here made me realize how much I missed her, how much I wished things could have been different. I didn't want to screw that up now. She had been alone for so long. I imagined it must have been torture to be in the city by herself, never able to show anyone who she really was. What could that do to a person? All the tension that must have knotted up inside her, all the shame and the fear of being caught, and with nobody to confide in either? My pity turned to admiration as I thought about all she had endured for the sake of her son.

"You're right. I don't have kids. I just don't like the thought of anyone having to hide who they are. When I think about you in the city all these years having to hold it inside and push the urges deep down I just... I don't know if I could do the same thing. But you're back here now, Kira. You don't have to hold it in any longer. You might not want to tell Deke about all of this, but that doesn't mean you have to hide it from yourself as well. You never know, letting go again might make you feel better," I said with a wicked smile. Her lips flickered as well and I knew that there was still something of the old Kira left in there. She hadn't been completely buried by the city.

However, she wasn't exactly eager to give me a positive reply either.

"I'm not saying you have to do anything drastic, I'm just saying that maybe you should come with me to the ridge tonight and we can have a race. I think I might have a good chance to win now after you've been through all this. And would you deprive a man the chance to end a humiliating losing streak?" I asked, hoping that my playfulness would break through her hard exterior.

For a few moments she stared at me and I thought she was going to shut down and shut me out again, that she had spent years building this grim barrier around her and was not about to let anyone else in, even someone she had known for years and years. But then her eyes shimmered with delight. I knew she would never be able to resist competition.

"I could stop being a dragon for a hundred years and still beat you," she said.

"Then prove it. If you've still got it then you don't have anything to fear. I'll be at the ridge this afternoon, around three. Meet me there and we'll see how much you remember."

"Okay," she said, "three it is." She folded her arms across her chest and gazed at me with that same steely look she always had. I was glad that she was at least able to stomach spending time with me, and I hoped that in time she would soften. There was so much I wanted to know about her time away from our home, so much I wanted to tell her, and it all needed time and patience. I was almost tempted to tell her that she could bring Deke if she wanted, but I had a feeling that would be too much.

"Well, enjoy breakfast. If you need anything else just let me know, and I'll see you at three," I said, deciding that it was a good time to make sure I did not overstay my welcome. I dipped my head towards her and called out a goodbye to Rock, before taking my leave.

Chapter Seven

K ira
    I watched Gordy leave with mixed feelings churning in my stomach. I was annoyed with myself for being goaded into a race. Shifting into a dragon after all this time wasn't exactly something I wanted to do, but Gordy had always been the kind of man who was hard to refuse. He had been a good friend before, although in the final moments he proved who he was truly loyal too. Perhaps if he had sided with me and turned on Tristan then things would have been different and I would never have had to leave here... but he and Tristan had always been tight.

I finished unpacking the last of the supplies he had bought for us. As a peace offering went it was a welcome one, and I started to make breakfast. As I did so Rock came out and told me to stop, that I was a guest and he was very capable of making breakfast himself. This was despite him having a hacking cough and having moments where he was unsteady on his feet. I told him to sit down, but he wouldn't listen. I ended up having to settle for him helping me, and I was glad breakfast was a simple meal.

"So, what did he have to say for himself?" Rock asked.

"He was just trying to welcome me home, I think," I said.

"Is that so."

"Yeah."

"Well, that's Gordy for you. He's a good lad."

"He can be."

"Kira, don't be like that. He always came to check on me and spend time with me. He helped out here as well. Without him I don't know what a lot of us old timers would have done." Rock said. I knew what was implied. That Gordy had to help him because I wasn't around.

"It's not my fault that I couldn't help you, Dad. Tristan made me leave."

"I never said a word."

"It was implied."

"I'm not saying anything," Rock said, holding up his hands in mock surrender. I rolled my eyes. Sometimes I felt that all the men here were impossible. We went to the table and started eating.

"Where's the kid?" Rock asked.

"I'll let him sleep. It was a long day yesterday. I want him to catch up on his rest. By the way, I'm going to see Gordy again this afternoon. I was hoping that you could watch over Deke."

"Sure thing, it'll be good to have some time alone with the little guy. I've got a few years of grandfatherly wisdom to catch up on," he said, and I didn't miss the slight arch of the eyebrow as I mentioned that I was going to see Gordy. I didn't comment on it though, and he knew better than to follow that thread of conversation too.

"Just no talk about dragons," I said, glancing over my shoulder before I mentioned the word in case Deke had managed to sneak downstairs without me realizing it.

Rock sighed and sagged in his chair. "Are you really sure about this, Kira? It's a part of who we are. It's a part of Deke's heritage. I understand that you don't have much fondness for the way you left this place, but does that mean he has to suffer? At some point he's going to go through the same change we've all been through, and when he has his first shift he's going to want answers. He deserves answers. If you don't prepare him it's going to be a terrifying prospect for him."

"I'll tell him in good time," I said sharply. "Obviously, I know that I can't keep it a secret forever, and I'm not planning to. I just want him to enjoy being a boy for as long as he can without making his life complicated."

"Alright," Rock said, remaining unconvinced. "It's just that he's going to find out at one point or another around here."

"And I'm going to be the one to tell him. I'm his mother and he deserves to hear it from me," I said in a tone that suggested this was the end of the matter. Rock pursed his lips and nodded, choosing not to pursue the matter further.

"So, tell me a little more about the last five years. Was there anyone I should know about in the city?" he asked.

"What do you mean?"

"A man."

I let out a scoffed laugh. "I've had my fill of men, Dad. I told you anyway, I couldn't afford to let anyone get too close in case they found out what I was. It was easier to be alone. Besides, I had Deke. He was enough of a handful."

"I see," Rock said, and he had that certain look on his face that all parents had at some point, a look that drove me crazy because he acted as though he knew something that I didn't.

"Come on then, Dad, say what you're going to say," I said.

"Well, I'm just a little confused really. You tell me that you don't want to meet anyone in the city because you can't tell them the truth about who you are, but then you don't want to be with a dragon either because of what happened. So if you can't be with a pure blood human and you can't be with one of your own kind then who are you going to be with?"

I sighed because it was something I had thought about during many lonely nights in a cold bed, and there was only one inescapable conclusion. "I suppose it means I'm not going to be with anyone," I said.

The heartbreaking look in Rock's eyes affected me more than I knew. "That makes me really sad, Kira."

"Why? It's my life."

"I know, but you're my daughter. I wanted your life to be filled with happiness and love, and I wanted you to experience the same kind of life I had with your mother. That was over all too quickly," he sighed again, "I just never imagined that you would be like this, that's all. There's still so much of your life left to live and to think that you're already giving up on it-"

"I'm not giving up! I'm just making a decision that is best for everyone involved. It's not as though my romantic history is any good, and Deke would be better off without all the upheaval in his life. It's just easier this way. It's better."

"You keep telling yourself that, but I know what this is really about. You were just the same as a child."

"What do you mean?" I asked, furrowing my brow.

"You never liked going back to anything that caused you pain. Do you remember when you were learning to fly and you crashed into that mountain? It took you years before you took that route again. And what about when you had that bad reaction to the gumbo I made one time? You never ate it again. I love you, Kira, and part of loving someone is being able to see their faults and tell them when they're wrong. Kira, you've always been averse to pain. When something hurts you, you tend to avoid it until you're ready. I get it, it's a survival thing. I've known many people who are the same, but when it comes to something like this you can't just ignore it. You can't ignore who you are, and you can't condemn yourself to living a life alone because you've been hurt in the past. You're too special for that. You have so many qualities that make you an amazing person, and I don't want you to miss out on anything in life. Besides, what are you going to do when Deke gets old enough to live his own life? You're going to be left behind again, and I don't think I'm going to be around at that point to keep you company. The worst thing in life is when you look around and realize you have nobody left. I don't want that for you."

"I appreciate your concern, Dad, but I'm going to be fine," I said, although I wore a mask. The truth is that his words did get under my skin. There had been many times over the years when I had felt the pangs of loneliness and wanted so badly to feel the comfort of being with someone again, but it was all so complicated.

I couldn't think about it now anyway. I had other things to worry about, like Dad himself, and Deke, who I heard stirring upstairs.

I went into his room and kissed him. He was sleepy eyed, but looked rested. "I got a little scared when I woke up Mommy. I forgot we weren't at home."

"I know, but you'll get used to it. Look at the view, isn't that better than looking out and seeing nothing but buildings?" I asked, gently lifting him into a sitting position where he could see the gorgeous expanse of desert stretching out, as though the world was new and simply waiting for something to grow in the vast desert. It was beautiful, and I had forgotten how much emotion it could cause to swell within me. I remember so well the sweeping mountains and the endless skies... so many things that had seemed so far away when I was in the city. Being home for just these brief moments had brought back so many emotions it was difficult to deal with them and I dearly wished things hadn't been so complicated.

Deke nodded, although I wasn't sure if he appreciated the grandeur of what he was seeing yet. I ran my hands along his back and my throat tightened. I knew it was only a matter of time before wings would grow, breaking through the flesh. I remember the first time it happened to me, how painful it had been. Even though Mom and Dad had sat me down and told me all about it and that it was just a natural thing I still wasn't prepared enough. Deke knew nothing of this. I had to tell him. I was going to tell him, I just didn't know how. Because telling him that meant telling him about his father, and then I was so afraid that Deke was going to want to learn more from Tristan, and that I could not abide.

I swallowed those feelings and kissed him on the head. "Why don't you get dressed and then come downstairs for some breakfast. Your grandfather is waiting to meet you. He is very excited to spend some time with you. Later on today I need to run some errands, okay? So you're going to stay here. But it's okay because your Grandad has lots of games and has lots of stories to tell you, and I won't be gone long," I said. Deke nodded. I let him get ready and then waited for him downstairs.

THE DAY PASSED FAIRLY quickly. There were moments when Dad seemed distant, as though a fog had appeared in his mind and he was lost to us for a few moments, but this always passed and he said that it happened occasionally. It was a little worrying and I made sure to keep an eye on it. He seemed to be getting on well with Deke though. They had a natural bond that was good to see, and as Dad taught him some card tricks I wondered if I had actually done Deke a disservice by preventing him from having a male role model in his life. I had always thought that I was enough for him, but had I been wrong? As a parent it was always difficult to fathom making a mistake, because any mistake seemed as though it was going to ruin a child. I had to remind myself that Deke was my child, and that meant he was as strong as me.

When it came time for me to leave, Deke ran up to me and hugged me tightly. I promised him that I wouldn't be gone long and the time would fly. I reminded him that he had to behave because his grandfather was poorly, and then I walked outside, ready to meet Gordy.

We met at a ridge we used to hang out at all the time when we were younger. It used to be the three of us, me, him, and Tristan. He was already there, sitting in the sun, baking away. Sweat trickled down my temples and the bright sun was glaring. I raised my hand to shield my eyes. The air was dry, the desert dusty under my feet. It cracked as I made my way up to the ridge.

"I'm glad to see you didn't chicken out," Gordy said.

"I've been gone a long time, but I haven't changed that much," I said as I joined him at the crest of the ridge. "It seems as though this place hasn't changed either."

"No, it's still beautiful," he said with a tone of reverence in his voice. I followed his gaze as he looked out over the world. The ground was made up of different shades of grit and sand, shifting from purple to tan to red, making it seem as though an artist had been busy with a varied palette. The mountains rose in sweeping grandeur, rising elegantly from the ground and towering impressively into the sky, which was azure and free of clouds. There were squat formations of rocks as well, looking like tables that giants would use for great banquets. I closed my eyes for a moment to enjoy the silence.

"I'd forgotten how quiet it is out here," I said softly, each one of my words a tiny blow from a hammer that cracked the fragile stillness of the world out here, a world that was far from the hustle and bustle of the city.

"Not what you're used to? I guess it must be different from the city."

"It is," I said. "There's always some kind of noise going on there. It could be neighbors banging around upstairs, or cars rushing by, or cats screeching. There's never any rest for anything there. Someone is always awake. Something is always happening."

"That's humans for you. They can never stay still and appreciate the world for what it is. They're always buzzing around."

"I guess that's why they've built all these cities and spread across the world while we still have our small settlements."

"Well, it also helps that there are far more of them," Gordy said with a smile. I nodded. I had forgotten how easy it was to talk with him. He had always been a good friend. I used to feel bad for him because Tristan and I were usually so caught up in each other that Gordy got left behind, but he never complained. He was a stalwart man, to a fault really if you consider what happened with Tristan. "So, shall we do this?" he asked. "We can head out to Spear Mountain, first one that makes it to the top wins," he said, pointing in the direction of a long, thin mountain that tapered to a tip, hence the name. It was a common route for us to race, and one that had been etched in my mind.

"Sure," I said, with nerves swimming in my stomach. It had been five years since I had left here, five years since I had last shifted into a dragon and flew away with a baby in my belly. When I arrived in the city I shifted into my human form and never left it. There had been moments over the years where I felt the urge, but I had always buried it down, like an addict who tore himself away from the pill that would have given him so much relief.

"Are you okay?" Gordy asked when he noticed that I wasn't shifting. There was a moment of doubt in my mind as I wondered if I was actually going to be able to do it at all. A part of me just wanted to walk away and leave this all behind. But two things played on my mind; one is that I did not want to do that in front of Gordy because he never would have let me forget it. The other is that I remembered what Dad had said about me being averse to pain. It wasn't the example I wanted to set for Deke, and I didn't want to spend my life living in fear either. I nodded and then breathed in deeply, summoning the primal energy that swirled inside, accessing the hidden part of me that I had ignored for so long. There was a moment when I thought it wasn't going to respond, when I thought that it was going to be angry with me for having ignored it all this time and it was going to resist my call, but it had no choice but to obey.

I had forgotten the pain though. It blazed through me, making my entire body tremble. The magic pulsed through me, making my flesh tingle before it was ripped apart and transformed into scales. I felt the fire in the pit of my belly, scorching me. I doubled over, collapsing to my knees in pain. Tears stung my eyes, my eyes that shifted to golden orbs and were better able to cope with the light from the sun. I felt my jaw stretching. Fangs grew through my gums, and I whimpered with pain. But the whimper wasn't that of a human woman, it was a guttural sound, one that sounded like cracked glass. I felt strong too, strong enough to move mountains. Then the wings came. I flung my neck back as my body arched, the wings extending from my back, feeling as though they were being extracted from me. My mind reeled and I wasn't sure if I could cope with the pain at all. I thought I was going to faint. But then it was over.

I tilted my thick neck and looked at myself. I saw my three clawed hand first. It had been a long time since I had seen the pale blue scales covering me, just as much a part of me as my other form was. I tilted my head to see Gordy standing there. His scales were a faded yellow, close to the color of sand. He flicked his tail and gestured with his head to Spear Mountain. The race was on, and I suddenly felt alive again. Exhilaration burned through my soul and despite my reservations I realized how much I had missed this. I flapped my wings and felt myself leaving the ground. My head soared with delight as I felt the air rushing around me, as I reclaimed my soul, as I remembered what it was to be a dragon.

Chapter Eight

T ristan
    Where was Gordy? He was never around when I needed him. No matter. I had been thinking about my last conversation with Kira and how angry she was at me. I suppose that was a better thing than her being indifferent. It was just a shame she had that interfering old coot with her as well. Rock had never liked me, because he was one of those who didn't understand me. Sometimes I wonder how I had ever fit into this place at all when there were so many people who didn't grasp what was possible. All I wanted was to make our lives better, and Rock was one of the ones who should have understood because then he wouldn't have to suffer through his illness any longer. All we had to do was follow the ways of Black Fang and things would have been better. One thing I didn't understand was why the Ancient Ones had been so against his philosophy in the first place. Were they that afraid of losing their link to their human form? I admit that there were some advantages to being human that could not be replicated in the form of a dragon, but we're talking about immortality here, and what could be more valuable than that?

Still, it was only a matter of time before I got my hands on my son. I wasn't going to let Kira or anyone else keep him from me. I had a right to him, and she had already managed to sever my bond with him for five long years. But now she was back and I was going to prove to her that I could be a good father. He would understand my goals. He was my blood, of course he would share my ambitions. It was just a question of getting some alone time with him, but surely Kira wouldn't be so cruel as to prevent him from spending time with his father?

Well, she probably would. She always bore a grudge against me for how we left things. It wasn't my fault though. She was the one who could never see the wisdom of my actions, and why should I have been happy with the way she was treating me? She was the ungrateful one.

I rubbed my temples and shook my head. I had never imagined life would be this complicated when I was younger. In the heydays of our romance, Kira and I had to worry for nothing. I still remember how things began between us. It was impossible to forget, and the thoughts had plagued me for so many years.

IT HAD BEEN A NIGHT where there were a thousand stars on display, as though they knew something special was going to happen. I had been feeling some tension between Kira and I for a while. It felt as though we were in a powder keg that was primed to explode. We made secret plans to see each other, away from everyone else. Rock never liked her sneaking out, but he could never stop her. She was too crafty for that. We met at our ridge and shifted into dragons as soon as we saw each other. She was so beautiful, her pale blue scales shimmering in the moonlight as though they were alive with color. With a flick of her tail she commanded my attention, and the way her body curved... I knew I had to have her. We flew through the night. I chased her, allowing her to stay just out of reach because that was the game we were playing. But then we reached the shadows of a mountain, hidden from the rest of the world. We hung in the sky, gently flapping our wings to maintain our altitude, staring at each other, drifting closer together with every moment that passed.

Our tails were the first things that touched, wrapping around each other. The green shade of my scales perfectly complemented her blue ones. We grew closer together. Her scales pressed against mine. My huge wings enveloped her and she nuzzled into the crook of my neck. Gently we descended to the ground, shifting back into humans as we did so, and our bodies were entwined, our flesh pressed against each other, burning with heat and desire. She looked up at me and I will never forget the wonder in her eyes. It didn't seem as though anything could be greater than what I was experiencing in that moment. All I wanted was her. All I could see was her. It was intoxicating and overwhelming and my hands never left her body, nor did my lips leave her mouth.

MY HAND CLENCHED INTO a fist as I brought it down on the table, annoyed at how beautiful things had seemed in the beginning and how darkly they had turned out. It never would have been that bad had she just been able to see sense. The worst of it all was that she was my mate, the mother of my child. I had a claim to her and she should have been by my side. She should have been loyal. Even after all this time there was still a stirring in my heart when I thought of what we had shared. The burning of blood was still present within me and I hated every minute of it because she made me feel so weak.

Gah!

I lashed out, swinging my arm around and knocking the wall. The house shook. My cheeks were flushed and the world was bathed in red. Never had there been another woman who had made a man so enraged. Never had there been someone who had been so adept at getting under my skin. I don't understand how she did it, how even after being away from this place for five years she could still have this effect on me. I would have done anything for her. I shared all my secrets with her and what did she do? She called me crazy. She called me insane. She said that I was a fool for believing the old stories, but I would show her. I would prove to her that everyone else was a fool for not believing me, and when I found Black Fang my son would be beside me whether she liked it or not. Deke was my blood and he deserved to have Black Fang's blessing as well.

I turned to the table where I had my documents spread out. The maps were drenched in ink as I had scrawled over them. I saw the way Gordy looked at them. Even he was beginning to doubt me. I bet all he saw were mad ramblings, but they made sense to me. It was in the depths of the cave where the answers lay. All I had to do was get there and Black Fang would be waiting. He had been waiting all this time for me, only for me. Then I would never die and I would laugh at all of them.

I stared at the maps and started to work out how many supplies I would need and what I needed to take with me. It was not going to be an easy journey. Black Fang wouldn't have made things easy. Only those who were most worthy would have been able to find his lair and get the answers to the questions that were so important. Only those who deserved his wisdom would benefit from it. I would just have to get Deke first though. I needed to see what kind of boy he was and if there was enough of me in him, for I was certain that his mother would have diluted plenty of it. Five years with her would have been enough for him to lose his way. How I pitied him, and how I hated her for keeping his true nature away from him. Was she ashamed of who she was? Did she look at herself with disdain every time she passed a mirror? Deke deserved to know his birthright. It wasn't fair that she was keeping his heritage from him. I was his father and I wanted him to know, and there was no way I was going to let Kira stop me from doing that.

It was time we had a proper conversation, just me and her, where we could lay things out properly. I didn't need her father interfering, and I didn't need Gordy trying to talk me out of it either. I would wait until the night, yes, because the night always meant so much to us, and then we would discuss our plans for Deke.

She had kept him from me for long enough already. It was time that he met his father.

Chapter Nine

G ordy

She took off like a lightning bolt. For a moment I had been distracted by her beauty. In both human form and dragon form she was gorgeous. The pale blue scales came alive as the sunlight danced upon them, and her elegant body curved in a pleasing manner. It was easy to see how Tristan could have fallen so madly in love with her. I couldn't imagine there was a man alive who did not desire her. I wondered about those in the city, those mortal humans who did not understand the depth to her soul or all she could offer.

But I had no chance to think about this either as she was already a body span ahead of me and I was determined to beat her this time. In all the races we had before she had beaten me. She was a natural at gaining speed, but she had just gone five years without embracing the dragon within her and this was my chance to show her that I was not going to be beaten again. I grit my fangs and flapped my wings at an even greater speed, using them like oars through the air, pushing myself forward. I managed to keep up with her. I watched her tail straighten like an arrow and then she flattened her wings against her body, becoming so lean she might as well have been a straight line. Suddenly she accelerated away from me. I had no idea how she was always so adept at finding the air currents. It was as though she had some insight into the sky that had escaped the rest of us. She could always sense where the pockets of air were so that she could avoid those that would slow her down and use the ones that gave her an uplift. I tried to follow her movements, but I was always a flap of wings behind her.

I felt the air rushing under my body and then she spread her wings, so I spread mine too. We rose up high and higher as the ground disappeared below us. I could feel the sun on my scales. Kira twisted and then burst forward. I had no idea how she did it. I tried to mimic the movement, but it didn't work in the same way and I only succeeded in losing precious seconds. I righted myself and instead of relying on the same tricky movements as she was doing I used my power instead, getting as much speed as I could from my wings and hurtling myself forward to close the distance between us. As I caught up to her I saw her glance back. There was a wicked gleam in her eyes and I realized she was enjoying being a dragon again.

Well, that was something I supposed.

We approached Spear Mountain. It rose impossibly tall and rushed towards us, its shadow cast long against the desert. Kira was already climbing through the air, twisting and turning, almost jumping between the different pockets of air that she used to elevate herself and assist her in ascending to the top of the mountain. This was my chance to catch up with her. It had been so long since she had been a dragon that she must have lost something in the way of stamina, so I summoned whatever strength I could muster and propelled myself forward, not caring to follow her route. Instead I barreled forward in a straight line, directly to the top of the mountain. I didn't even glance her way as my eyes were locked on the dark, jagged rocks. The air whipped against me and as the shadow fell over me I felt the coolness caressing my body. The top of the mountain was so close... so close... there was the plateau, a smooth slab that we always used as a landing platform. It was within my sights now and I hurtled towards it, willing to crash if I needed to, all to beat her. I could feel that it was happening. After all these years, all these defeats, I was finally going to beat her. I reached out, preparing to feel the stone crashing against my body, when suddenly I sensed the flicker of movement beside me.

No.

It was impossible.

How had she managed to catch up to me?

I roared with dismay as I crashed to the plateau, only to realize that she landed at exactly the same time as me. I rolled around, my impact sending me crashing into a wall of rocks. The impact was thumping and the air rushed out of my lungs, while she sat there gracefully, perched there as every movement of hers had been deliberate, and she had been completely in control.

We both shifted into our human forms. I brushed pebbles and dirt off me, wincing as pain radiated through my bones.

"So I think I just got a tip of a claw on the mountain before you," I said. She tossed me a glance and arched a disbelieving eyebrow.

"I'll give you that we landed at the same time, but that's as good as it's going to get, Gordy. Besides, I think I deserve extra points for the landing. You seemed to crash there," she said.

I walked towards her and then sat down beside her. Our legs dangled off the plateau. The world was far below us, as though we were the only two people in the world.

"Okay, well, it was more of a controlled crash. But that was closer than it was in the past."

"It was, and that's with me being out of action for five years. I don't think you're going to get that close again."

"Well, we'll have to have another race at some point. Maybe I can learn how to navigate the skies like that. I still don't know how you do it," I said, looking out into the blank air, wondering how Kira could see so many things that were blind to me.

She shrugged. "It's just a sense. It's just the way my mother taught me."

The mood turned a little somber at the mention of her mother, but I was glad to see she was in good spirits.

"So admit it; you enjoyed that, didn't you?" I asked.

She turned her face away from me. "It was certainly an experience. After not doing it for five years there were certain feelings that I had forgotten and the rush of excitement was something that had been lost in time."

"So that's a yes then," I replied with a smug smile.

"Fine, yes, I admit it. I enjoyed it, okay? It's been a long five years," and then she shot me a warning glance, "but that doesn't mean I'm going to make this a regular thing, and it certainly doesn't mean that I'm going to change my mind about Deke."

I held my hands up to protest my innocence, as if to say that I wasn't going to bring Deke up if she didn't want to bring him up. I had brought her up here in the hope that she would remember something of what it was like in the past, before all this drama happened. I didn't want to remind her of the things that made her sad.

"It feels like a long time since we were up here together, doesn't it?" I said. "I used to love it up here, coming away from everything else, just looking out at the world and not seeing anything else for miles on end. Don't you ever miss that in the city? It must be so busy. I can't imagine being around that many people. Is there ever any privacy?"

"Not really," she said with a sigh, "but you get used to it."

"I think sometimes you can get used to too many things and settle for the way things are. Kira, I just want to say that I'm sorry for the way I acted when this all happened. I kept telling myself that it was just a fight and eventually the two of you were going to calm down. I never thought you would actually leave. I always thought you'd come back. I... I missed you."

I suppose I hoped she would say that she missed me too, although if she felt that way then she didn't say it. The whole matter was complicated because of her history with Tristan, but I had to try and separate my friendship with her from my friendship with Tristan.

"Did you never even think about it?" I asked when she didn't say anything.

"There were times when I looked up at the night sky and I wondered if I was doing the right thing, but then I would go into Deke's room and look at him sleeping. He was so peaceful without knowing about any of this and I didn't want that to change. I would do anything to protect him, even if it means giving up something that was a big part of my life."

"Have you thought about what's going to happen if he decides he wants to stay here?" I asked.

"I don't know yet. I don't think I'm going to be around here long enough for him to like it that much. I'm going to makes sure that Dad is stable and then I'm going to head back to the city."

I frowned, for I hadn't expected her to be this steadfast in her dislike of this place. "But what about today? Don't you feel any differently now that you've been a dragon again?"

She placed her hand against her head and spoke with forceful words. "I can't afford to feel differently. Deke and I have a life in the city. It wasn't exactly my choice to leave, remember. Tristan was the one who wanted me to go, and if he says that he wants me to stay now then he's just a hypocrite."

"He did love you," I said in a small voice.

"He had a funny way of showing it," she swept her hair away from her face. I gazed at her profile, looking at the slant of her nose and the swell of her full lips. Yes, it was indeed hard for any man to not desire her. "I just can't deal with all this Black Fang stuff, Gordy. When he first spoke to me about it I thought it was just some hobby he was indulging, but he's gone full into the conspiracy and I can't have Deke exposed to that. He doesn't even know dragons exist for goodness' sake! I just want to get in and get out and then my life can go back to normal."

"Except it's not normal, is it," I said. I was beginning to get tired of her continually disparaging our way of life, as though we should have been ashamed of who we were. Up here there was nowhere for her to escape either. "At least not for us. We're dragons, Kira. You can't just turn off that part of you. You even just admitted that you enjoyed accepting that part of yourself again. Why should you have to life as half of yourself if you don't have to? I'm sure you and Tristan could find a way to work it out. I'll help you. I'm still your friend."

"Are you?" she turned her head to look at me directly. I saw defiance and fury and fear in her eyes.

"Of course I am," I said. I know we had had our difficulties and I know five years had passed, but it hadn't changed the way I felt about her. I couldn't believe she would ever doubt it, but I suppose being away from us for so long had had many negative effects.

"Then stop telling me what to do or how to act. It's my life and I get to live it in any way I choose. I know what's best for my son and I'm going to raise him accordingly. If you want to keep spending time together while I'm here then you're going to have to stop speaking to me as if I don't know what I'm doing."

"Okay," I said, an edge to my words. We settled into silence as we stared into the beauty of nature. I wondered how someone I had known so well could turn into this being filled with bitterness and tragedy. Part of me wished that I could go back in time and act differently, support her when Tristan had threatened her with exile. Maybe she had a right to be angry with me. I just wish I knew how I could have made it up to her. A lot of time passed with us sitting there in silence, but I think perhaps we needed it, just to get used to being in each other's presence again. Eventually I took a risk and spoke up, hoping that it wouldn't elicit another harsh reaction from her.

"It was good to see you in action today. You haven't lost any of your skill."

"Thank you," she said. "I do appreciate you doing this, Gordy. It has been a long time and it... I hadn't realized how much I had missed it. I don't think it's going to be the last time I'm going to shift into a dragon while I'm here."

"Good, I'm glad to hear it. I just want you to be happy, Kira. It's what you deserve after all that's happened. I just wish it could happen here instead of the city," I said.

"I need to ask you about Tristan. I thought he would have gotten over this obsession by now. Why has it gotten so bad?"

I shrugged and picked up a smooth pebble, turning it over in my hand. I idly tossed it away, watching it soar through the air before gravity clutched it and dragged it down into the abyss below us. "he just can't let it go. Every time someone gets ill or dies he starts to think about his own mortality, and he keeps thinking that he's running out of time. I've tried to get him to stop, but he just won't. He's convinced that he's found Black Fang now. The thing is he's never going to stop looking. In his mind Black Fang is out there, but look at how much of the world there is to explore. It's all a fool's errand, but maybe I'm the fool for letting him continue with it. We've just been through so much together. I can't let him go through this alone. If I do that then I've truly lost him."

"Maybe it would be better for everyone if that's what happened. If he wants to find Black Fang then fine, go and find him, just leave everyone else out of it."

I wasn't sure there was ever going to be an end to her bitterness, and it put me in a difficult situation. It was even more complicated because part of me believed she was right. If Tristan wasn't around then perhaps Kira would stay, and if she stayed then maybe things would be different.

Before I could say anything else she rose to her feet and said that she had been away from Deke for too long. We turned back into our dragon forms. This time there was no race. We flew back in a straight line, and as I veered away home I wondered whether I was right to give my loyalty to Tristan. What if by doing that I was actually missing out on something wonderful myself? I was going to have to ask myself some difficult questions, and I wasn't sure I was going to like the answers.

Chapter Ten

Kira

    I flew back home, shifting back into my human form became I came into view of the ranch. The last thing I wanted was for Deke to see me like this. I had no idea how I was supposed to explain it to him. I had much on my mind, and despite my initial misgivings I had to admit that being a dragon again was freeing. I had forgotten how wonderful it felt to fly through the air, to feel the wind rushing past me and caressing my body, to see the world from a new height. I had missed out on so much the past five years, and I realized that I had suffered through the barren spell. Somewhere along the way I had convinced myself that I wanted this, that it was a choice I had made, but after being a dragon again I knew that had been a lie.

    Damn Gordy for challenging me to race him after all this time. I should have stayed strong and stopped myself from falling into the trap, but what a trap it had been. A smile played on my lips as I thought about flying up Spear Mountain, of dancing through the air and finding the small pockets that helped give me a speed boost. The lessons my mother had taught me were lodged deep in my mind, and I wondered if I wasn't actually doing Deke a disservice. Being a dragon and being taught how to be a dragon had enabled a strong bond to be formed between myself and my parents. Was I depriving myself and Deke of that bond by hiding his true nature from him?

    I shook the thought from my mind, deciding that I didn't want to think about it. Instead I thought of Gordy. There were times when he drove me crazy with his questions, but I knew they were coming from a good place. There were so many times over the years when I thought about what my life would have been like had I fallen in love with Gordy instead of with Tristan. At least Gordy wasn't obsessed with some myth. But then Deke wouldn't have been born. There would have been some other child in his place, and as much as I hated Tristan for the way he had treated me I had to accept that without him Deke wouldn't have been born.

But being with Gordy had also shown me that I had forgotten what it was like to be with someone else my own age. In the city I had kept everyone at an arm's length. Even with people I called my friends I never let them past a certain point. With Gordy, I could be myself, and I had forgotten just how freeing that could be. I suppose that I could spend a bit more time with him before I would inevitably leave, before I had to turn my back on this place again and return to a world that didn't want anything to do with me.

When I returned home Deke leaped up from the table and ran to hug my legs. I picked him up, which was still something I was just about able to do, although given the way he was growing I knew it wasn't going to be long before he would be too heavy for me.

"Did you have fun?" I asked.

Deke nodded. "Grandpa taught me how to play cards!" he said.

I glanced at Rock, who shrugged as if he had been helpless to resist the urge.

"We only played with pennies," Rock said.

"I don't particularly want my child to develop a gambling habit this young," I said.

"I did the same thing with you and you turned out fine. Did you have fun?" he asked with a knowing look. Deke was still unaware about everything of course.

"I did, actually. It felt nice to be with a friend again."

"I'm sure it did. Gordy is a good lad, you know, and he hasn't settled down yet either."

I rolled my eyes. Sometimes Dad could be so transparent.

"I wouldn't know about that. We didn't talk about his love life. Or mine, for that matter. It's almost as though we know to respect each other's boundaries," I said with a pointed glance. I wasn't sure if Dad gleaned the deeper meaning to it, or if he just didn't care. He waved a hand in the air.

"You kids think you have all the time in the world, but you don't. Soon enough there will come a day when you realize that the best days of your life are behind you and it all would have gone like that," he snapped his fingers as he spoke and looked entirely disheartened. I wondered if I would ever be like that with Deke, disappointed that he couldn't see what I knew. I'm sure there was some wisdom in my Dad's words, but the thought of romance was so far from my mind that I didn't even want to consider it. All I could think about was Deke. I wanted him to have a good life, an untroubled life, and the best way to do that was limit the number of people in that life because people only ever made things more complicated than they needed to be.

I spent some time with Deke in the afternoon. He moaned a little that there wasn't as much to do here as there was in the city. I told him that I would take him for a walk outside the following day and he could see the beauty of the world.

"I know this place may not mean so much to you right now, but it is where I grew up. There was a time when I was just your age you know. I used to run through this ranch and outside and I would..." I trailed away as I remembered the memory, how I skipped along the ground, shifting as I did so, so that on my final skip I leaped into the air and soared away. I couldn't say that to Deke though. I had to keep it a secret. I ruffled his hair and I told him that he would get used to life out here soon enough, and that one day we would be back in the city.

AFTER DINNER DEKE WANTED to play cards, to show off the things he had learned from Dad. I was happy to spend some quality time together so we had a few good games, and Deke had learned all the same tricks that Dad had taught me. We pretended to be caught by surprise by them though as it made Deke feel like he was outsmarting us, and sometimes the best thing for a kid was to feel smarter than the adults around you. When the night settled in I led Deke upstairs and put him to bed, kissing him on the forehead as I told him I loved him. I ran my hands along his back again, knowing that eventually the day was going to come when I would have to tell him who he really was, and what he was capable of. I wished there was a way for him to stay a child forever though. Being a child was easy. Growing up was always the most difficult thing in the world, and it could never be avoided.

As I set him down to rest and watched his heavy eyelids close, I sensed something behind me. I looked around and out of the window, and then I saw him. His green scales looked sickly in the moonlight, and his eyes stared directly at me. Anger rose in the pit of my stomach as I drew the curtains, shielding Deke from the world outside, and then I stormed out of the ranch. Rock asked me where I was going, but I didn't have the patience to tell him.

How dare Tristan come here again after I had told him to stay away. How dare he continue to goad me after he had made me leave in the first place.

The air was cool outside, the beauty of the world hidden as darkness came upon it as though a blanket had been draped across the world. Tristan had already shifted back into his human form, looking so smug and certain as always, as though he had all the answers that anyone would ever need.

"What the hell do you think you're doing here? I made it clear already that I don't want you hanging around here, and you certainly can't just show up unannounced and hover outside my son's window. Are you trying to undermine everything I'm trying to do? I want to protect him, Tristan," I said, somehow managing to keep my voice to a hushed whisper, although it was impossible to keep it from being terse.

Tristan sounded calm, which was even more annoying than if he had been irate. "Why would you want to protect him from himself? It is his nature. Our nature," he said.

"It doesn't matter why. What matters is that he's my son and I'm raising him as I see fit."

"He's our son," Tristan said.

I laughed out loud and paced around, flailing my arm in the air as rage ran rampant within me. "Oh no, you are not going to do this, Tristan. Just because I came back here does not mean that you suddenly have a right to see your child. If you wanted to see him then you could have been a father to him, but no, you got angry and you wanted me to leave."

"Because you wanted to see sense!"

"There's no seeing sense with you. You want to chase Black Fang? Fine, go for it, but don't drag me into it and especially don't drag your son into it either. This doesn't have anything to do with him. He doesn't deserve to be a part of this life. I'm warning you now that you should stay away and-"

He stepped forward, the sudden movement distracting me and cutting me off.

"I know you hate me, Kira. I acted rashly. I did not expect you to call my bluff and leave. At first I did not think I needed a child in my life. But after seeing him, after these five years have passed I feel as though there's a hole in my soul. I am a father whose son doesn't know anything about him. How is that supposed to make me feel? All I'm asking for is a little time to spend with him."

"You ask too much," I spoke coldly. All I wanted was for him to leave.

"You should feel fortunate that I'm asking you at all. I'm well within my rights to walk in there and tell him about me. He's my son."

"You didn't want him when I told you about him. What were your words exactly? Oh yeah, you thought he was going to be a distraction from your studies. You were already at the point where I was a distraction. You could barely bother with me. It took everything I had just to get you to look at me. And then I fall pregnant and you get angry with me? No Tristan, no, you don't get to make me out to be the bad guy. This is not happening."

Chapter Eleven

Tristan

I gazed at her as she spat those bitter words at me. I could smell the anger on her. This raw emotion... I shuddered at the intensity. It had been so long since I had felt this way. It reminded me of when we were young, when she had intoxicated me with her alluring desire. It had been so easy to fall into her back then, to lose myself in her scent and her smile and the way she cocked an eyebrow in that teasing way, somehow shrugging off all the world in such an innocuous gesture. She had been so coy once upon a time, deceptively so. I always thought she was a quiet girl, a thoughtful girl, but then the first time I had her alone she showed me the fire that burned within her. She showed me her passion and her heat, and now she was showing it to me again.

Five years. It had taken me five years to miss her. Now she was back, with my son, and I wasn't about to let her leave again. I could see the hatred in her eyes, this fury that burned as brightly as our fiery breath and I knew that she still felt something for me. She might not have been able to admit it to herself, but it was still there. I smiled and sneered and looked smug.

"I'm not trying to make anyone out to be bad, but as far as I can remember you had plenty of bad moments back in the past. You must remember when we flew to the lake. The whole desert was bathed in our screams. I still have the scars from your claws that night. You didn't want to let me go. It's not possible to forget moments like that," I said.

Something flickered in her eyes. I knew she hadn't forgotten. She had been my mate and she always would be. We were bonded beyond anything and it had only been a matter of time before she returned to me. I would ensure that she never left again.

A smile curled on my lips. "You do remember, Kira. I imagine you have been thinking about it all the time in your absence. You might have been able to move away from this place, but you would never have been able to leave it in your heart. This is your home, and you have been away for too long. Let us begin again, Kira. Fate brought you back for a reason."

"Fate had nothing to do with this. I don't know what kind of twisted image you have of me in your mind, but it's got nothing to do with the reality. The reality is that I left because of you, and the only thing that brought me back was the love I have for my father. But I guess the bonds of family isn't something that means anything to you, is it? You don't understand it, and I pity you, Tristan, I really do. But here's one thing you're going to have to get in that thick skull of yours. I'm not your family. Deke isn't your family. You have no place here so stay away," she grit her teeth as she spoke her words, forcing them out of her mouth as though each one of them was a knife that was going to stab me in the heart. I wasn't scared though. It only served to amuse me how she would fight with herself to deny the truth that was so plainly evident. Let her believe this fairytale, because soon enough I would show her the truth.

"Okay, Kira, okay, you have it your way. But you can't hide from your true nature for long, nor can you stop Deke from learning about it too. At some point he's going to want to know about his father and I'm going to be here to teach him everything he needs to know. But I think there are a few things you could learn as well, or remember at least. It's such a shame that you haven't embraced your dragon side since you left. Why don't we go for a fly? It'll be just like old times, you and me in our own little world, dancing among the stars," I said.

She smiled, and for a moment I thought she might actually be willing to listen to what I had to say. But then she opened her mouth again, and I realized that I had been betrayed.

"Actually, Tristan, Gordy beat you to the punch. We already went to Spear Mountain. It was actually refreshing to feel that way again. And it was nice to spend time with a friend, rather than with someone I would rather forget. I'm going back inside now. I suggest you leave the premises before you make my father angry. I know what great respect you have for older dragons, and I'd hate for you to have to go against your core beliefs," she said.

Anger coiled within me. I watched her walk back inside as my blood boiled. What was Gordy doing spending time with her when he knew how much she meant to me? Was she lying? Perhaps... but there was something in her tone that suggested she was telling the truth. She and Gordy had always been close. It wasn't beyond the realm of possibility, but why would she have flown off with him and not me? She and I had more history together.

I wasn't going to learn any more from her though. Meeting my son would have to wait, but I was not going to wait forever. In time I would have him stand by my side and learn all about Black Fang and the destiny that awaited us both. In time, Kira would see that the greatest mistake of her life was when she walked away from me.

GORDY LOOKED SURPRISED when he opened the door. I walked inside, not waiting for him to invite me in.

"Why are you surprised to see me, Gordy?" I asked, scanning the room to see if she had been in his ranch.

"Well, it's just been a while since you've paid me a visit. Usually it's me coming to you."

"I thought I would change that. Friends should spend time in each other's houses, after all," I said, and decided that I wasn't going to play coy or try to goad the truth out of him. "I spoke to Kira today."

"Oh yes? How did that go?"

"It was illuminating. I caught a glimpse of my son as well, through the window. I hadn't realized how much his absence had affected me. To have him so close to me and yet not be able to see him... it makes me realize everything I have missed out on. I wish I could have done something differently. I wish I could have spent more time with him, but I suppose he's back now and I can make up for all the time we have lost. At least I would be able to, if there wasn't one person standing in our way."

"Kira," Gordy said.

I inclined my head. "It seems as though her heart has not recovered from the past, and now she's poisoning my son against me. This cannot be allowed to happen! I will not allow her to leave again with Deke, not within us having a proper conversation. Deke needs to know his birthright. He needs to know what he is. The thought of him living in that human world never knowing his true potential... it sickens me," bile rose in the back of my throat and the world turned an ugly shade as I thought of the life my son must have been living. How ordinary Kira must have taught him to be, how mundane the lessons he had been taught were... my hands curled into fists. "I may need your help, Gordy. She has committed a crime of the severest nature and I will see that justice is done. You are my oldest friend. You know me better than anyone else and I know that I can always count on you. Will you help me spend time with my son?" I asked, my eye twitching as I examined him carefully.

I noticed the sharp intake of breath and the look of guilt upon his face.

"I mean... I want to, Tristan, but I'm not sure it's really my business. Isn't this more of a family matter?" he said.

"But you are family, Gordy. I've always seen you as my brother. You're the person I trust most in the world..." I let my words hang in the air. I watched the emotions ripple across his face. He was torn, no doubt between me and her, but there should have been no decision. I was his friend. I was the one who had stuck by him all these years.

"What's wrong, Gordy? Why do you hesitate?" I asked, my words teasing and needling. If he was going to betray me then I wanted to make him squirm. I wanted to make him do it like a man. He stared into space, clearly searching for something that would save him. But there was no salvation. I sighed as I paced towards him.

"Gordy, I know what happened today," I said.

"What do you mean?"

"I know that you saw Kira. I know that you went to Spear Mountain with her. I have to say that I was quite surprised. I didn't think you enjoyed spending time with her so much, but I suppose you always did have a soft spot for her in the past, didn't you? It's just that, well, you know how precarious things are between us right now, and how the fate of my son rests in the balance. I'm sure that you were only spending time with her to tell her how she needs to be more forgiving towards me, and while I appreciate your efforts I'm afraid I'm going to have to ask you to not spend any more time with her. She's back here, and I should be the only person she's spending time with. I'm never going to form a connection with my son if I don't show her that it's the right thing to do."

I expected him to apologize profusely and tell me exactly how he had erred, but instead he sighed and pinched the bridge of his nose. It was in that instant I realized he had turned against me. Somehow she had managed to turn him against me.

"Tristan, look, I get what you're saying, but I think you're going about this all wrong. After what happened she's really hurt, that's all. If you just apologized to her and started off at a basic level again then maybe she'd be more likely to give you the time you need. But you have to ask for it and appear humble rather than make these demands. And this talk about Black Fang... it's not doing you any favors. You know she never liked it in the past so why do you think it's going to make any difference now? I think maybe you need to forget about Black Fang and focus on the things that are important to you. If that is Deke and Kira then take the time to be humble, maybe help her out with Rock, just be like a regular person."

"But I'm not a regular person. I'm a dragon, and I have more important things to do than what you ask. I'm disappointed in you, Gordy. You should have sent her to me if she wanted to reclaim the dragon inside her. She is my mate and that is something I should have witnessed."

"She stopped being your mate the moment she left," Gordy said in a small voice. I narrowed my eyes and I could barely stop the anger from coursing through my blood.

"What did you say?"

Gordy sighed and tilted his head back. "Look, you know I like you, Tristan. You're my oldest friend, but even I have to admit that I think you're going pretty far with this obsession with Black Fang. I'm only telling you this for your own good you know, but things aren't going to end up the way you want them to just because you demand it or because it makes sense in your head. Kira is a person with her own feelings. She's been hurt. She's the one who has been taking care of Deke all these years and I don't think she's going to change that just because you want her to. You're going to need to think of a better way of going about things."

I regarded him in silence for a few moments as I let his betrayal sink in. "I don't know what she said to you to make you feel this way, Gordy, but I do find it disappointing. I thought you were going to be a better friend than this. All I want is your help in reclaiming my mate and my child, but if you wish to stand against me then so be it."

"I don't want to stand against you, Tristan," Gordy said, flinging up his hands and shaking his head in disbelief.

"You may not want to, but that's exactly what you're doing. You're supposed to be my friend. I suppose I have seen this coming for a long time. I should have known something like this was going to happen when you lost your enthusiasm for Black Fang. It's a shame that it has to come to this, but now I need to give you a command, Gordy. Stay away from my mate. Stay away from my child. I don't need you interfering in my affairs," I said, my voice calm and cool. I gazed directly at him so that he could be under no illusions as to the convictions of my soul. He stared at me open mouthed and barked a laugh, as though he couldn't believe this was actually happening.

"You can't be serious, Tristan. You can't order me around. You can't tell me who I can and can't see. Kira was my friend too you know, or have you really forgotten everything we went through in the past?"

"I haven't forgotten," I said, stepping forward towards him, "no, I haven't forgotten at all. I haven't forgotten the flash of envy in your eyes when I went off with Kira. I haven't forgotten how you always used to stare at her even when you thought I wasn't watching. In a way I'm proud of you for finally embracing your feelings towards her, Gordy, but you're too late. She's already been claimed and I'm not going to release my claim on her yet."

"Tristan, you're speaking about her as though she's some object. She's a woman. You can't tell her who she can and can't spend time with, just as you can't tell me the same thing. If I want to see her again then I will. I want to be your friend, but you're not making it easy on me."

Anger flared. I felt the flame licking every part of me. I lashed out, punching him in the jaw. He hadn't been expecting the blow so his head snapped to the side and he cried out in pain. How dare he try and blame me for all of this. How dare he try and say that I was being unreasonable.

Gordy stared at me again. This time he wasn't going to use his words, just his hands.

Chapter Twelve

G ordy
    I stared at him, my best friend, my brother, but it was as though I was looking at a different man to the one I had grown up with. Who was he to place demands upon me? It was the first time I realized that he had lost his mind. In all this obsession with Black Fang he had lost himself, and now he was deluded enough to think that he had a right to Kira and Deke? No, this wasn't the man I called my friend. This wasn't anyone I wanted anything to do with.

Then he hit me. The shot came from nowhere. Pain blazed across my jaw, but I felt the shock more than anything.

I snarled and threw myself at him, grabbing his neck and trying to drive my fist into his chest. We wrestled through the house, sending each other into the walls. I managed to drive him to the floor, taking his legs out from underneath him and I thrust my fist into his gut. He choked on his breath, but my punches did not have the impact they needed because I wasn't able to get enough back lift. I grunted as he lifted a knee and slammed it in my lower mid section, causing me to lose my grip on him. I rolled off and he leaped up, kicking my chest. I scrambled for the couch and used it to leverage myself up. Tristan tried to strike me with his elbow, but I managed to evade the blow at the last second and turned around, punching him in his face. I heard the sickening crack of his nose and blood trickled across his lips. We grappled again and pushed each other around, both trying to gain supremacy over the other, both trying to gain the advantage. My muscles burned. Tristan had always had so much inner strength, and the fact that he was a couple of inches taller than me really told in a grapple like this. I grit my teeth and battled against him as he slammed me into the doorway. He brought his hand back and punched me again, but I ducked and his hand hit the doorframe, splintering the wood and making the whole ranch shudder. I bowed even lower and then speared him with all my weight, sending him clattering to the porch. We rolled down the steps, the two of us feeling the jagged impact of the steps in our back before we landed on the dry, scratchy ground.

I pushed myself to my feet and was a hiccup quicker than Tristan. I sent a powerful jab into his face and watched him shake it off. He scrambled back. Now that we were outside we had more room. We circled each other, staring at each other.

"Are you sure you want to do this, Tristan? There's no way back from this. You ruined things with Kira before, do you really think shedding blood is going to make her think any differently?" I yelled.

"It doesn't matter what she thinks! This blood is dragon's blood. She cannot deny this is who she is. This is what she belongs to," he said, and as if to illustrate his point he stretched his arms and embraced the dragon within. He shifted before my eyes, turning into that jade form he was so proud of. His tail flicked through the air as he flapped his wings and lifted off the ground. His jaw opened wide. If he had breathed fire then my human flesh would have been charred beyond recognition. His fangs glinted in the dim light. His claws were sharp, ready to dig into the world and tear it apart. If this fight was going to continue then I knew what I needed to do.

I inhaled and shifted too, feeling my skin cracking into scales. The world blurred for a moment as my eyes changed, and once I regained my vision I saw him hurtling towards me. He sank his claws into my tough hide and I arched my neck back as I howled in pain. He flapped his wings and we ascended from the ground. He twisted and gouged my skin. Dark blood oozed out over my yellow scales as I struggled to break free of his grip. I wriggled and writhed. The pain was intense, but necessary. A huge gash was torn across my skin as I wrested myself free, and kicked him away. I braced myself against the pain and took a moment to process all the sensations that were coursing through my body. Tristan hovered in the air for a few moments, sent off balance, but then he was flying towards me again like a missile. This time I was able to counter his movement and quickly dodged out of the way. I twisted, blood dripping through the air and splashing on the desert ground like rain, and slashed at him with my claws. I caught one of his wings and he howled in pain. I then flew underneath him and looked up, targeting his belly. I bared my fangs and my claws, ready to tear him back down to earth before his tail came thundering in and swatted me away, hitting all the wind out of me from the side. I lost my balance and spun out as he came barreling and butted me with his head. I was sent flying back and as the world spun I had to try and orient myself.

My wings flapped frantically and I managed to get above the ground, just as he came steaming towards me, his eyes glowing with fury. I took the blow, tensing my muscles at the perfect moment to brace myself against the pain. I shot back quickly, this time drawing some blood myself. His bestial hiss was a scorching scream and I knew he was out of his mind. He tried to hit me again with his tail, but I caught his tail with mine. They were entwined as I struggled to keep his away from me. We were straining so much that our bodies trembled. He swiped at me with his claws and then twisted back, still gripping my tail with his, as though he was diving backwards. He pulled my body with it and my head spun as I lurched forward. As I realized what was happening I spread my wings and fought back, trying to catch the air to stop him from wrenching me, but it felt as though I was being pulled apart and I had no choice other than to unwind my tail from his.

The moment I let go he surged up towards me and caught me with the full force of his body. Tristan had always been the better fighter. He was more vicious. I hung in the air and needed a moment to catch my breath, so I turned away from him and flew as fast as I could. The mountains loomed up from the ground, getting closer and closer every time. My wings were tired and I could taste blood in my mouth. I groaned as I saw him like a shadow behind me, shifting from side to side, like a hunter that was waiting to strike. I prepared to lay a trap. I acted more wounded than I actually was and let my wings sag, falling a little through the air. Then Tristan approached me and prepared to make a killing blow, but as he did I twisted around and dragged my claws along his flank.

He spasmed and lashed out at me with everything he had, catching me on the side of the head. I was knocked back again and then I realized he had caught hold of my tail in his claws. He moved so quickly it was impossible. He held me tightly and before I could flap my wings to stop the motion he was already swinging me around, sending me hurtling against the wall of a mountain. The impact made my bones shudder and I coughed up blood. Still Tristan wasn't done. He pummeled me and clawed at me and scratched me, and then he took my head in his hands and spat blood at me. I weakly flailed against him, trying to fight back, but the fight had all drained out of me in my slick and viscous blood. He gave me another few punches for good measure and left me sinking down to a slab of rock, heaving in breath as he flew away, his shape a dark shadow against the night sky.

I lay there, defeated, demoralized. I coughed up blood. My wounds stung. I pushed myself to my feet and tried my hardest to regain my balance. The look in his eyes... he had gone mad. I couldn't believe that he had been that savage towards me. He could have killed me if he wanted to, and perhaps it was only the history we shared that had stopped him. Or maybe it was just the fact that he knew he would be beyond redemption in Kira's eyes if he had killed me. I knew he wanted to. I could smell it on his breath. I gasped and grunted as I limped away, my wings flapping slowly. I clutched my wounds as I flew back to try and gain some kind of equilibrium after this humiliation.

Tristan may have won this fight, but he was going to lose in so many other ways.

Chapter Thirteen

K^ira

    Anger was still rushing through me and I couldn't sleep. Tristan had always been able to get under my skin. I hated him reminding me about our youth because it made me think about when I actually did love him, when I would have done anything for him. I was just a stupid naïve girl back then though. I liked to think I was wiser now.

Deke and Dad were both sleeping. I wanted to crawl into bed, but what was the point? I would only have been tossing and turning like most other nights since I had left. I was shaken by a knock at the door. At first I was annoyed because I thought it would be Tristan again, but then I realized that Tristan wouldn't have knocked.

I flung the door open to see Gordy standing there. He was in his human form, clutching his side. Blood trickled from the corner of his mouth and his face was bruised. He looked as though he had been hit by a juggernaut.

"What the hell happened to you?" I asked.

"Can I come in?" he wheezed, his breath a rapid gasp. He stumbled inside. I looped my arm around his body to steady him and showed him into the kitchen, where I poured him a glass of water and fetched a first aid kit. In the light his wounds looked even worse. His skin was a shade of purple where the bruises lay.

"Okay, what is this, Gordy?"

"Tristan," he said. My eyes widened at the horror of what he was saying. Tristan had always been the type to stand tall for his beliefs, but to attack Gordy like this was something else. Gordy was supposed to be his friend and if he was capable of this then he really had lost his mind over the last five years.

"He did this?"

Gordy nodded as he sipped the water. "We got into it. He came to see me and said he wanted my help to get you back. I told him that he needed to stop demanding things of you and just tell you how he felt, how important it is to be a father. But he wouldn't listen. Then he started talking about how I had betrayed him and how I shouldn't spend time with you, and how he should have been the one to help you reclaim the dragon."

I choked on a gasp. It was partly my fault. I had goaded Tristan with the fact that Gordy and I had gone off flying without realizing how Tristan was going to react. I dipped some cotton wool in antiseptic and began to clean Gordy's wounds.

"Anyway, I told him what he didn't want to hear and then he hit me. So we got into it, ended up throwing me into a damn mountain," Gordy continued, his dry laugh turning into a choking cough. I told him to hold still because I accidently pressed my finger into a gaping wound. He winced in response.

"I'm sorry for telling him that we had gone off together," I said.

"It's not your fault. He didn't need to react like this."

"Was he always this crazy?" I asked, trying to make a joke of the situation to make it more light hearted. Gordy wore a serious expression though.

"He changed when you left," he said.

"When I left?"

"Afterwards he wasn't the same. He was in shock. I don't think he ever expected you to stand up to him like that. He kept saying how he was going to track you down in the city, but he never did. He went out at night, searching for you, but I guess you got too far for him. Then he just got even more obsessed with Black Fang and now I'm not sure if I'm ever going to be able to reach him again." Gordy shook his head.

"I let him down. I always let him lead. I should have been stronger. I should have told him to stop."

"It's not your fault, Gordy. Tristan has always done whatever Tristan wants to do. If he had been able to get out of his own head then he would have been able to see that what he was doing was wrong. He can dress this up anyway he likes, but in his world he's always going to make other people out to be the bad guy, and we don't have to stand for it. He shouldn't have treated me the way he did, and he definitely shouldn't have treated you this way either. I don't know why he still thinks he has a shot at being Deke's father. I don't want him around my son."

"I know... sometimes I wonder why you even fell in love with him in the first place, but I guess he was always the most daring one, the strongest one, the one who could fly the farthest. I remember how the two of you never had any fear. There were no boundaries you couldn't cross, nothing you wouldn't do for each other. I always thought you two were meant to be."

As I listened I noticed a wistful tone in Gordy's words. Even back then I had known that he had feelings for me. To be honest there weren't many other females around our age, and with how close he, me, and Tristan were it was basically a shoot out between the two of them. Gordy had always been the kind of guy to hang back, to wait a second too long. In my youth I had been attracted to Tristan's daredevil attitude. There was never an adventure that he would not go on. Every day was always exciting with him and at the time that's what I wanted. He used to take me to the mountains and talk to me about the ancient dragons and how we were the superior race, and I ate it all up. I was a fool back then.

"Well, I long stopped believing in destiny," I said as I continued to tend to his wounds. The fight must have been a savage one. Part of me wished that I had been there to stop it, but it was more likely that I would have gotten involved. I noticed him wincing and touching his side. "Take your top off," I said.

"Aren't you going to buy me dinner first?" he said wryly, although his smile gave way to a wince of pain. I sighed a little and shook my head at his poor attempt at humor, and then watched as he pulled his shirt over his head. He revealed chiseled muscles and the feminine part of me twitched inside. I felt a tightness in my throat as I looked at his tanned skin, the broad chest narrowing to a tight stomach and waist, with a dusting of hair rippling across his muscles. It was a display of real manliness, of strength and heat and in my five years of celibacy my appetite had grown to the point where hunger gnawed inside. I always had to keep men in the city away, not just for Deke's sake but also because I could never allow them to get to close, to learn the truth about my nature. Gordy knew it all though. I didn't have to hide myself here.

The only thing blemishing his perfect skin was a long gash that stretched across his stomach. It would heal in time. That was one of the benefits we had as dragons, but it still looked painful. I touched it tenderly, the tips of my fingers pressing against his supple flesh. He was warm, and there was a pulsing rhythm underneath his skin. I found my gaze lingering on his body and I had to tear it away, for I didn't want to show him that I was being weak. But as I did so I looked up and caught his steely eyes, and he knew. Oh God he knew. I went about tending to this wound, cleaning the area before placing a long bandage over the gash, running my hands over his body, trying to ignore the tingles and tremors that were running through me. He sat there silently, his chest rising and falling in steady breaths.

"Why did you do it, Gordy? Why did you stand up for me? You could have told him what he wanted to hear. You could have stood by him again, just like you always used to do."

"Maybe I'm tired of standing by him. Maybe I see that he doesn't deserve my loyalty. Maybe I want to make up for the past. That day still kills me, Kira. I thought you were going to come back. I waited for you. I thought you were going to return and when you didn't I knew that it was as much my fault as it was Tristan's. I should have spoken to you, sided with you. I was blinded by loyalty for my friend, my brother... I should have realized that some things were more important. I should have seen the path he was going down and I... I'm sorry that I realized it too late. I'm sorry that you felt so alone."

I listened to his words carefully and embraced them in my heart. I had waited a long time for someone to say that, and it meant a lot coming from him. Now that his wounds were dressed I went to the cooler and fetched a couple of beers, then jerked my head for him to join me out on the back porch. We leaned against the porch, gazing out into the starry sky.

"To be honest, I think leaving was the best thing for me. I couldn't have raised Deke here, not with Tristan around."

"It must have been so tough though. You must have been so lonely."

My head dipped and I sighed. I raised the bottle to my lips and took a long gulp, hoping to numb the sharp feelings that usually stabbed at my insides, and that it would give me the courage to be truthful. It had been so damned long since I had had a conversation like this with anyone.

"I was, but I got used to it," I said.

Gordy looked at me. I could tell he didn't believe me. Maybe I didn't believe myself.

"I've been lonely too," he said softly.

"You've had Tristan, at least."

He chuckled at that.

"Hasn't there been anyone that's caught your eye then? Nobody passing through that you wanted to keep for yourself? I know this place is quiet, but there must have been someone over the years," I continued.

"There's only ever been one," he said. Even though I wasn't looking at him I could feel his gaze bearing down on me with its intent. I could feel the heat of it simmering my skin. I almost dared not look up, but over the years my courage had not been dulled. I gasped as I met his gaze, seeing something in his eyes that I hadn't seen before. It was exciting and scary all at once, and it made my stomach twist in knots.

"Be careful what you say, Gordy. You might never be able to take it back."

"I might never be able to get the chance either, Kira," he said. "I waited too long to say it before and then you left. If I don't say it now then maybe you'll leave again. Maybe I'll have to live my life always wondering what might have happened if I had just been honest with you. You know it already, don't you? You've always known it. You can't have escaped the way I used to look whenever you and Tristan went off together, how I was always the one left behind, always the one wondering if it would ever be my turn to find something like you guys had. You must have seen the way I stole glances when I thought you weren't looking. God, I was so tense around you, always afraid that you would discover how I really felt. Hell, sometimes I wanted you to see it so badly, just so that the pain would go away. It was torture feeling that way about you, Kira, because I knew that you were Tristan's, and I certainly wasn't going to fight him to the death for it. I wasn't the dragon you needed. And I guess maybe when you left I sided with Tristan because it was some way of getting revenge against you. It's twisted, I know, and I'm sorry. I thought I had left all this behind me. I thought I had let the pain go away but then from the moment I saw you in the diner it came flooding back. It had just been buried deep down inside me and there was nowhere for it to go.

I still feel that way about you now, Kira. Somehow you're even more beautiful than you were before, but you still have that fire. You still have that spirit. Going up to Spear Mountain when it was just the two of us I..." he trailed away and I used the opportunity to stop him. the words rushed around my head and danced, intoxicating me along with the beer I was drinking.

"Gordy... I'm also a Mom."

"I don't care about that. Deke seems like a great kid, and he's got so much of you in him."

"My life isn't here."

"We don't need to talk about what's going to happen in the future. We just need to live in the moment. That's what you were always good at doing, weren't you? I know I wasn't as reckless as you wanted a guy to be back then, but maybe that's a plus point for me now. Is there really nothing inside you that's pulling you towards me?" he asked.

I could have lied and told him no. It probably would have been the easier answer and it would have saved me a lot of trouble, but I had left so much behind when I had gone to the city with Deke. I had to shut down parts of myself that I thought I would never feel again, and being around Gordy made me want to embrace them. I could feel the stirrings inside me. He wasn't the same Gordy that I used to know. Or maybe I wasn't the same Kira I used to be. Tristan had always been the one to catch my attention, but now it was Gordy in the foreground. He was reliable, dependable, he was good, and maybe my life could have used a dose of good.

So in response to his question I didn't say anything. I stepped closer towards him, placing my free hand on his chest. There were mere inches between us. I tilted my head back to look up at him. Tension made the air burn. I rolled forward on my tiptoes and he caught me with a strong arm. I tasted the beer on his lips. I felt his tongue dancing in my mouth. I felt years of desire swelling inside him, and years of loneliness being burned away inside me. It was a hard kiss, a kiss that had been in the making for years, and I knew it wasn't going to be the only kiss we shared. Something was beginning here, something that I couldn't ignore. Hell, I had lived a long time in the wilderness. For the first time since I had returned I thought it was good to be home.

"Let's go away somewhere tomorrow, just the two of us. We can talk more, have a proper date. Maybe we'll go by the lake again," Gordy said.

I found myself nodding. Then I smiled. It felt as though a weight had been lifted from me. Suddenly it was easier to breathe and the world seemed new, and I felt hope for the first time in a long time.

Chapter Fourteen

Tristan

I had a long time to think about things after my fight with Gordy. I returned home to lick my wounds and recover. It took until the following day. I could not let this betrayal stand. He was going to poison Kira's mind against me, just as she was poisoning her child's mind. Deke's place was with me. There was nothing she could say to convince me otherwise, and deep down I knew she believed it too. My blood ran through his veins and I had a right to see him.

And I would see him.

He would understand what I was trying to accomplish. My son would know. I went to my table and looked at the map of the mountains I had placed upon it. All these years of searching and I was finally close to my goal. I was finally going to be able to find Black Fang, and what great timing it was for Kira to return because my son could be by my side when I found him. I almost trembled with anticipation, but there was one final part of my plan. I had to actually find a way to get to Deke. Kira would never let me, no matter what I said, so I would have to wait and watch and then strike when the opportunity presented itself to me.

Once I found Black Fang then everyone would realize that I had been right all this time. I doubted they would actually be humble enough to come and apologize to me, but perhaps they would do me the dignity of letting me into their lives. It baffled me how Kira could live in a city with all those humans, focusing on the weakest parts of her, trying to turn my son into something that he wasn't. It made bile rise in my throat. He was a dragon and he needed to be taught about his legacy.

Dawn rose. I lay on top of my ranch with a pair of binoculars. I had a direct line of sight to Rock's ranch. During the morning I saw Gordy and Kira emerge. From their body language I knew that something had happened, something that I found distasteful. No matter. She had left me a long time ago, and it wasn't her that mattered anymore, it was only Deke. Although I did find myself thinking about the way Kira had always been so fearless, so daring. There were times when her passion even worried me. She had been so spirited... I thought we were soul mates, but then she wanted me to set everything aside and be a father. Why couldn't she see that what I was doing was important? If I'm right then nobody needs to die. I would have thought she would have understood more than most people considering the condition of her father.

I sighed, trying to push the thoughts about her away from my mind. They often came back needling me, torturing me. I didn't understand why. She had been gone for so long. The five years apart had seen me get closer to my goal than ever before. It was clear I was better off without her, and yet still it irked me to see her and Gordy together. I still remember the way her body arched underneath me, and that sweet sigh that was so melodic as we drowned in kisses. Even now I swear I could smell her scent on the air. Those days seemed far away. I scowled. I didn't need to think about this. I only needed to think about Black Fang.

I watched them leave. They hadn't taken Deke. I was a little tempted to see where they were going, but it didn't matter. They were probably fooling themselves into thinking they had some kind of connection when the only thing they had in common was that they had both betrayed me. They would soon learn their lesson. It was time for me to strike.

I JUMPED IN MY TRUCK and the gravel crunched underneath the tires as I sped away, hurtling towards Rock's ranch. I pulled up and hammered on the door. Rock took his time answering, shuffling in that old man way of his. I winced, hating the idea of ever falling prey to the withering touch of time.

He squinted at me through his cloudy eyes.

"I thought Kira made it clear that you ain't welcome around here," he said.

"Well Kira isn't here, is she? I'm here to see my son," I replied, craning my neck past him to try and see Deke.

"That ain't happening. Just turn around and go back to your ranch. I don't want any trouble, but if you take one step into this ranch then I'll give you a reminder of what an old man can do." There was a glint in his eye, almost as though he was daring me to try. I was young, strong, and I had no doubt that I could defeat him in a fight, but where was the honor in that? Besides, old dragons had a wily way about them and I wasn't about to put myself in a position where I was going to be embarrassed. I stared at the decking. My foot was on the porch, an inch away from the threshold of the door.

"I don't want any trouble either, Rock, I just want to see my son."

"He may be your blood, but you ain't been no father to him."

"Because I was never given the chance," I hissed. "Do you think I wanted this? Don't forget it was your daughter who chose to leave. Are you telling me that you're fine with her decision? Are you really going to tell me that you've never once felt a sliver of resentment for her over the years? She didn't only take my son from me, but she prevented you from knowing your grandson."

"Well, she's back now," Rock said, although it was clear that he didn't disagree with me.

"Yes, she's back, but for how long? She's only going to take him away again. This is the one chance I have to meet Deke. You must know how precious that is. You at least got to see Kira grow up before you spent five years apart from her. All I want is a chance to know my son."

For a moment I thought my plea to his heart would have done the trick, but Rock shook his head. "I appreciate your position, maybe more than Kira does, but she's my daughter and I'm not going to go against her wishes. You'll have to talk to her. Once she gives the okay then you can come in, but not before."

I pressed my lips together tightly. "Rock, surely you can't agree with what she's doing. She's hiding our true nature from the boy. How is that going to help him when he starts to shift? She's not doing him any favors. He needs a father to teach him the kinds of things that only a father can teach him," I said. I could see in Rock's eyes that he believed me, but he was still so loyal to his daughter. Damn Kira, she had everyone wrapped around her finger.

But I quickly learned that I didn't have to convince Rock.

"Who are you?" a voice called out from behind Rock. I looked past the old man and saw what appeared to be a younger version of myself. It was uncanny. I saw so much of myself in him. A smile widened on my face while at the same time bitterness filled my heart by the fact that Kira had stolen five years of time that I could have spent with him. Ah well, I thought, if I was successful in what I hoped to achieve then we would have all the time in the world together.

I pushed past Rock, ignoring his warning about coming in, and crouched down so I was on the boy's level.

"Well Deke, I'm Tristan, and I'm your father," I said.

Deke tilted his head as he processed the words. It was a huge bombshell to lay on a child, but he was a dragon. I was convinced that he could handle it.

"My Dad?" he asked.

"That's right. I know we've never met before and I'm sorry about that. You've been living in the city, and I've been out here. But I've wanted to meet you for a very long time and I'm glad that we finally have the chance. Have you been wanting to meet me as well?" I asked.

Deke wore an uncertain look as he slowly nodded his head.

"Well good!" I said. "Look, while your Mom is out running errands would you like to spend some time together? I'd love to get to know you more and learn all about your life in the city. I'm sure I can teach you a few things about life here as well. It may not be as glamorous as life in the city, but it has its charms. Do you like the mountains? They're impressive, aren't they?"

"Yeah," Deke said, his words still curt, his heart still unsure. Without the reassurance provided by his mother it was right that the child should be scared, but I would soon see to that.

"Well, what do you say, do you want to go and spend some time together? I promise I'll have you back in plenty of time for you to see your Mom," I said.

Before Deke answered he cast his gaze to Rock. I turned towards the old man too. "What do you think, Rock?" I asked. "Are you going to stop a man from spending time with his child?"

Rock sighed, knowing that he was in an impossible position. He relented, and told Deke to go and put on his boots. He took the opportunity to come up to me and thrust a finger towards me. "You take care of that kid, okay? If you hurt a hair on his head then all of us are going to come to you and tear you apart scale by scale. And you'd better bring him back because if you dare think of doing anything funny-" he only cut himself short when Deke returned, his laces dragging against the floor. Rock's message was clear in his eyes though. I protested my innocence because of course I wouldn't have done anything to harm my child.

"Let me get those for you, Deke," I said, and bent down to tie his laces. "We're just going to go for a little ride, okay? And I'll tell you a little bit about the history of this place." Kira wasn't there to stop me. Nobody was there to stop me from finally telling Deke about his birthright. The future was going to be mine... no... it was going to be ours. I took his hand and let him out to my truck, calling out to Rock that I would see him later. I smirked as I pulled away, knowing that I had scored another victory.

Chapter Fifteen

G ordy

My wounds still ached. The kiss I had shared with Kira had gone a long way to soothing my anguish though. I had stayed in the spare room the previous night after we had spent a good few hours talking. She was still so intoxicating, just the same as she had always been. Her eyes were as bright as the stars and her smile could light up a room. She was the kind of person I always wanted to be around, and I tell you what, the kiss we shared had been long worth the wait. My younger self must have been proud of me. And yeah, it was tough about what happened with Tristan, but sometimes things changed and there was nothing you could do about it. Tristan had made his decisions and it was time I made mine.

I fetched my truck and then drove us up to the lake. It was a short drive up a winding road that led to a wide oasis. The water was always warm because the sun shone upon it, and the ground was still dry around it. It was a place that had always been special to us though. I parked up and we got out, walking towards the lake. She wore a swimming costume underneath her dress, slipping it away. At first I thought she was stripping and my eyes almost popped out of my head. Damn did she look good though, still with her curves in all the right places, a figure that could make any man go mad. My wounds were healing up nicely. I peeled off my shirt and felt the sun kiss my skin. We dipped ourselves into the water, relaxing in the warm liquid. It shimmered and seemed to dance as the sunlight hit it.

"So have you still made it a regular thing to come up here?" she asked.

I nodded. "As often as I can. It still looks beautiful at night," I said. The lake grew cooler in the moonlight. I tried to push the thought out of my mind, but I couldn't forget how often she and Tristan had flown up here in the depths of night to make love. It was a long time ago, almost another life, but it was still hard to think about their history when I was trying to make a future with her. "I bet you don't have anything like this in the city," I added with a teasing smile.

She leaned back and laughed. "There certainly isn't."

"So what is it actually like, living in the city? I mean, I get that you haven't wanted to come back here, but there must be something keeping you there?"

"I mean, there's lots about it that's great, although it took some getting used to. But there's always a store open if you need anything, and there's always something to do. You can never get bored. I didn't realize how much I had gotten used to the noise though. Out here it's so quiet, you can really hear yourself think."

"I don't think I could handle the city then. I like these quiet nights. It makes the world a beautiful place. And as far as I'm concerned there's plenty to do around here."

"Oh yeah, well, you were always easily amused," she teased.

I chuckled. "There's nothing wrong with being a man of simple pleasures."

"I guess not," she said, nodding along. I stared at her, wondering what kind of life she had truly had for five years. There were some moments when it seemed as though no time had passed at all, and others when I could tell how haunted she was by what had happened.

"So has there really been nobody special? I mean, I get that you were busy with Deke, but surely at some point someone must have taken an interest?"

She took a few moments to answer. Maybe she thought I was trying to gauge the competition.

"There was one guy who came close. We worked together and he made it clear that he wanted to get to know me even though I had Deke. I liked it at first, you know, it was nice to be reminded that I was still a woman rather than just a Mom. But the closer we got the more I pulled back. There was one night when he told me a secret, something really deep that he said he had never told anyone before. Then he asked me if I had anything I wanted to tell him. I thought about this place, about who I really was and what Deke is going to turn into and I just... I couldn't. And I knew that's what my life was going to be like. There would always be a lie, and I didn't want that. It wasn't fair on him or anyone else, so I just came to terms with the fact that my life would be like this."

"It shouldn't have to be. Nobody should ever have to hide who they are," I said.

"In an ideal world," Kira replied. She kicked out her legs and made a splash, sending ripples shooting across the lake.

"I know you don't want to talk about this, so just tell me to shut my mouth if you like, but are you really going to keep Deke in the dark about who we are? Who he is?"

Kira leaned her head back, arching her body in a way that made her breasts stick out of the water. She spread her arms out and looked as though she wanted the lake to swallow her up and free her of her worries. Strands of hair became wet and clung to her skin, splayed across her shoulders.

"I know I need to," she groaned, "I just don't even know where to begin. I thought I'd wait until he showed signs of his first shift. Right now I don't know if he can even understand it. How am I supposed to tell him that he's part of an ancestral race of beings who can shift from a human form to a dragon form? And I don't want to burden him with the lie. It's not fair to him because he's going to want to tell his friends, but he can't. He doesn't understand the kind of danger he's in. So to protect him I have to lie to him myself and I know that one day he's going to hate me for it."

"I don't think he's ever going to hate you. How could he? You're all he's ever known."

She looked at me sardonically and had her eyebrows raised. "Are you telling me you never hated your parents? Dad and I have had our bust ups over the years. Frankly I'm a little surprised we haven't had one yet already. I guess it shows how sick he is..." her voice trailed away. I wondered if she regretted leaving and missing out on all these years with Rock. It must have been tough on her to leave so many things behind for the sake of being away from Tristan, and it made me more annoyed at him that he had forced her into making this decision. I was quickly beginning to think that it would have been better for everyone if he had just left in the first place rather than Kira.

"I'm sure it'll all work out for the best," Gordy said.

Kira looked at me and wore a slanted smile. "You always were the one to see the best in everything, weren't your Gordy?"

"I try. You know, there's too much sadness in the world. I get that we're blessed to be who we are, but in a way we're cursed as well. We don't get to live normal lives like everyone else, so we just have to make the best of it. I'm sure that Deke is going to grow up and understand everything you've done for him. If he ever does anything other than that then just bring him back here and I'll knock some sense into him," I offered, although it brought some pain to my heart as I was reminded that at some point she was going to want to return to the city again. Now that she was back in my life I didn't want her to leave it again.

"I appreciate that, although I'm not sure it's going to work. The hard way of life never really worked on me. Dad tried it all the time. He used to threatened to tie me to the bed because I kept sneaking out even when I was grounded," she laughed in a carefree manner. "It's crazy isn't it, how nothing seemed to matter back then. It was all just so free and easy and we never had to worry about anything. I don't know when it all changed, when it was that we all grew up. But now I look at my life and I see all the dangers of the world and I feel so much responsibility. I'd love to just go back in time and feel as though nothing mattered, but I guess maybe that was the problem. If I had the wisdom I do now then I would have done things differently."

"Like what?"

"I wouldn't have gotten on Dad's nerves so much," she said, "and I wouldn't have gotten into so many fights. I also wouldn't have allowed myself to fall in love with Tristan. I just... I couldn't see at the time how he was such bad news. I wish I had. I wish I had been smarter."

"You can't blame yourself. The two of you were good together. I always had the sense that you were going to end up together. You had that kind of energy, you know, when you look at people and just think that they fit."

I almost bit my tongue. I could have throttled myself. What the hell was I saying? After all these years was I still the same Gordy that put my own feelings aside for the sake of other people? Was I really trying to convince her that Tristan was the one she should have ended up with all along?

She looked back at me with those shimmering eyes of hers. They might as well have been as deep as the lake itself.

"You always did have a romantic edge Gordy. Have you ever found the person you fit with?" she asked.

I looked away from her, gazing at the horizon. I looked so far into the distance that I could not tell where the world ended and the sky began. It was as though I was looking into the past and the future all at once, to those impossible moments that would never come to pass again. I remembered the pain of having to watch Kira fly off with Tristan, always wondering what would have happened if I had just told her the truth about how I felt.

"I think I did find her, but I'm not sure she fit with me as well as I fit with her."

"Maybe it just needed time for her to find her perfect shape," she said. My gaze drifted towards her and as I looked into her eyes I thought I saw a sense of intent behind them. I wasn't sure if it was just wishful thinking on my part or if there was genuinely something there. Then she reached out to me and rested her hand on mine. The warmth of her touch was comforting and exciting all at the same time. She then lifted a hand and placed it against my cheek, her fingers touching the rough, scratchy stubble. It had been so long since anyone had touched me with such grace and comfort. I closed my eyes and a low murmur escaped my lips. Her fingers drifted across my cheek and then she shifted closer towards me, the presence of her body becoming clearer and more immediate within my mind. Her sweet fragrance drifted along the air and I was inured to her sweetness. I bowed my head towards her, my eyes still closed, moving on instinct more than anything else. I felt her warm breath flowing over my lips. We kissed, and it was as though a flame darted through me and spread like wild fire. My heart trembled and I was gripped with passion. My hand reached around the back of her head, her hair cascading over my fingers. I kissed her hard, almost as if to prove to myself that this wasn't some kind of dream or fantasy. This was really happening. After all these years we were together, just like I had always wanted. It was me instead of Tristan, finally, and she had been able to open her eyes and see me in a way she had never been able to see me before. It felt as though I was soaring so high I had touched the sun, and yet I knew that in time I would have to let her go again. She flicked and flittered through the world like a fairy, ethereal and impulsive and unable to settle. I felt as though I had to get as much as I could from her while she was here. The unbridled passion soared through my veins and I ended up pushing her against the ground. She laughed and threw back her hand, eventually squirming out of my grip.

"Don't get ahead of yourself," she said, laughing again. I withdrew, red faced, trying to loosen the tense knots that had tightened throughout my body, while also attempting to breathe away the passion that had been roused within me. She adjusted her dress and ran her hand through her hair, smoothing out some of the knots and the errant strands.

"I'm sorry I just..."

"You don't have to be sorry Gordy," she said with a reassuring smile, and then reached over to place a hand on mine. "I like it, okay? It's just a little much for now, you know, I prefer to take things slow."

I almost wanted to say that she had never taken things slow with Tristan, but I managed to bite my tongue. "I'm just afraid of taking things too slow, you know, because you're going to leave again."

The smile faded from her face and she turned away from me. I guess that had been the wrong thing to say.

She picked up a pebble and flung it across the surface of the lake. It fell underneath the surface of the water with a loud splash, and then the lake was still again. "I don't know what I'm going to do with my future, okay? All I know is that I have to do what's best for Deke. If that means leaving then I'll leave. If it means staying here then I'll stay. But I can't make any promises other than that."

"I get it. I do, believe me. I just... it's hard for me, you know. I missed out on a chance to tell you how I felt before. And now that you're back and we're here like this I just... it's hard to stop myself from getting excited. But I know that you're going to leave again and I'm going to be left behind again, except this time I'll really know what I'm missing out on."

"Would you rather we not see each other while I'm back?" she asked. I could sense she was getting defensive. She was sitting with her knees drawn into her chest and she stared at the ground. She had been away for five years and she was a Mom, but in some ways she hadn't changed at all from the girl I had once known.

"That's not what I meant, and you know it," I said, reaching out to touch her back. I breathed a sigh of relief when she didn't flinch.

"I've felt this way about you for a lot longer than you've felt this way about me. I have to protect myself Kira because I know it's going to hurt again. That's all."

"It's going to hurt me too. Life hurts. It's the one constant of everything, and one day Deke is going to have to be hurt as well. Maybe this was a mistake. Maybe I let myself fall too easily into this," she said as she got to her feet. I could feel I was losing her. Panic resided in my heart as I rose after her.

"Kira, come on, we don't have to be like this. It's going to be okay. We just need to talk about things, that's all."

"All anyone wants to do is talk. Is it too much for me to ask for something that I can actually enjoy without having to feel like I'm letting someone down? Or that someone is demanding too much from me? I came back here to look after my father Gordy, that's all. If something else happens then great, but I'm not sure I can give you what you want from me. That girl you knew is gone. She left here a long time ago. I'm not her and you can't put me on that pedestal again. I'm a mess, okay? Is that what you want to hear? I fell in love with the wrong guy. I guess things would have been much better if I had gone out with you all those years ago, but I didn't. I made a mistake and I paid the price. But it's not as easy as going back in time and fixing things. This isn't a second chance for us Gordy. This is... this is my life and I'm not just going to be the girl you remembered because it would make things easier for you. I think it's better if we just head back to the ranch and take some time to think about what we're doing. Maybe it's my fault. Maybe I took advantage of you. I'm desperate and your lonely and that's never a good combination. We've been through too much together to let it go like this," she said, and was already heading back towards the ranch.

I knew Kira well enough to not even bother to try and argue with her. There were so many things I could have said, but she would probably think I was trying to mess with her head. I wasn't that guy. I wasn't Tristan. I just wanted to love her, and she was the type of woman to make it so damn hard to do so.

We drove back from the lake in silence. She placed her arm on the open window and leaned her head out. Gravel crunched under the tires as I wondered if I had just ruined my one chance of being with her. I told myself that while she was still in this place I still had a chance, and I wasn't going to let her go so easily this time. She might have been adamant that she was going to leave again, but that wasn't written in stone yet. She said she was going to do whatever was best for Deke and so far in his life Deke had lacked a father figure. Tristan was far too obsessed with Black Fang to be a good father, so maybe if I proved to Kira that I could be that man she would see that she had more of a reason to stay here.

We made it back to the ranch and I intended to spend some time with Deke, but when we arrived I saw Rock standing on the porch, wringing his hands. I knew immediately that something was wrong.

Chapter Sixteen

Tristan

I looked down at my son as we drove along the dusty desert road. He peered out of the window, gazing at the natural beauty of the world.

"It's a hell of a sight, isn't it?" I said. He didn't turn to face me. "I bet it's a lot different to what you're used to." He nodded. "I think this place is more beautiful than the city. Man is capable of a lot of great things, but all these tall and ugly skyscrapers are nothing compared to what nature can do. I mean look at those sweeping mountains and the way the color of the earth blends together to create that purple shade. It's just beautiful," I said. I could wax lyrical about our environment all day. Of course, it looked even more beautiful from above, but I couldn't tell him about that yet. I had to ask him more questions. Kira had said that she hadn't taught him anything about the glory we hold inside our hearts, but the dragon inside is instinctual and I had no doubt that Deke had some inkling of what he could be, even if Kira hadn't told him.

I'm sure she was a good mother, but in this respect she had failed him and it was an error that I could not forgive.

Deke merely continued staring out of the window. "You know, I always hoped to meet you," I continued, "and I always wanted to bring you out here. I don't know how much your mother told you about me, or if she told you anything at all, but I never wanted to be a stranger to you, Deke. I do admit that when I learned I was going to be a father it was quite a daunting prospect. I had other commitments that I was looking to explore, and your mother just couldn't understand what I was trying to do. I'll explain it all to you though. I'm sure you'll understand better than she could. It's something that a father should pass on to a son anyway. She wanted me to stay away. That's the only reason why we haven't met yet. I'm sorry, Deke, but I hope that I can make it up to you now we're together. There's so much that I want to share with you, and we'll get to all that in time, but right now I think we should just spend some time getting to know each other. I'm sure this place is different to what you're used to, but that doesn't mean it's bad. It's quiet out here, reflective. The city has always seemed too busy. I bet it's noisy, isn't it?" I asked.

Deke nodded. So far I was a little disappointed that he wasn't more talkative, but I suppose that was something I was going to have to teach him too. Kira had really done him a disservice by taking him away from me.

"Well, out here you can really hear yourself think, and thinking is one of the best things anyone can do. It's important to reflect on ourselves and the world around us rather than being distracted by noisy and sparkling things. I love it at night when you can almost hear the wind whispering at you. Have you heard the wind whispering to you, Deke?" I cocked an eyebrow as I looked at him, wondering if he was going to show any bond with the land.

"I don't think so," he said. "But I have had dreams."

"Dreams?" I asked. "Are they scary dreams?"

"Kinda," he said.

"What happens in these dreams?"

He tilted his head to the side as he thought, and scrunched up his face a little. "I'm over the world. I'm flying. Like a bird. I keep thinking that I'm going to fall, but I never do."

Pride swelled in my heart as I listened to it. It had begun. Dreams were the first stage. It was only a matter of time before he would show his wings, before he would embrace the same primal essence that burned in all of us. Yes, with him I could find Black Fang. It was invigorating to have a son beside me, to know that we would share in this quest. Kira could not deny it of me. She could not keep me from spending time with Deke and sharing what made him so special.

"You weren't flying like a bird, Deke, you were flying like a dragon," I said, smirking as I drove the truck to the shadow of the mountains, leaving the small settlement behind.

I HELPED DEKE CLAMBER out of the truck. He gazed up at the impossibly high mountain and then looked back in the direction of his grandfather's ranch.

"Don't worry, we won't be out here for long. I'll have you back to your Mom before night falls. This is just something that I wanted to show you. It's been around for, well, as long as the earth, I suppose. It'll be around long after the cities have crumbled into dust as well. This is what matters in the world, Deke. Things that people build crumble and break, but what nature makes exists for a reason and it's so hard to fight against it. It's the same with us. There's a part of our spirit that is bound to this land and if we can embrace it and touch it then we can be like this mountain," I said, although he just stared blankly back at me. I suppose he was only five years old so I couldn't have expected him to understand everything I was trying to tell him, but as long as I planted the seed of the concept in his mind then it would grow as he grew, and he would ask the same questions of the world as I did.

I began to walk up the sloping path that led up the mountain and beckoned for him to follow me. He went slowly, his short legs only able to carry him so far.

"Tell me, Deke, how do you feel about your grandpa being sick?" I asked.

Deke looked towards the ground and shrugged.

"I know it must be difficult. After all, you've only just met him and already you have to worry about him. It's not fair for one as young as you to be burdened with these kinds of things. I hope that you're spending a lot of time with him though. Time is all too fleeting. I never got to spend enough time with my grandparents, or with my father for that matter. There were always too many other things to do and it's so easy to put things off for another time... but I digress. Let me ask you a question though, you know your grandpa is very sick, well, if there was something you could do to ensure that he never got sick again, wouldn't you do it? In fact, if there was something you could do to make sure that nobody else ever got sick again, don't you think it's the right thing to do?"

Deke thought about the matter for a moment, and then nodded. I beamed with pride. He was truly my son after all!

"This is why I needed to be around you sooner, Deke. There's something that has been missing from my life, and now that I'm spending time with you I am truly seeing what it is. I think I have found a way to do the impossible, but I need help. It's a treasure hunt of a sorts. Do you like treasure hunts?" Deke smiled widely and this time he nodded his head vigorously.

"Good, good," I said. "The only thing is that your Mom doesn't really like treasure hunts and she's not as convinced as I am, but let me tell you a story. You see, in these mountains there's a very old, ancient being who knows the secrets to save people. If I find them then I can learn these secrets too and we can help save people. Imagine that, your grandpa would live on and you'd never have to worry about losing your Mom either! None of us would have to lose anything," I said, trailing off a little as I thought about all the people I had said goodbye to over the years, all the people who had died when they didn't need to. Black Fang was out there and if we learned his secrets then nobody would ever have to suffer from death again. It was a shame that it took a child to understand the gravity of the situation, but at least with Deke by my side I could finally pursue my reason for being.

As we walked up the mountain I noticed that he was flagging a little, dragging his feet behind him and panting.

"It would be easier if we could fly, wouldn't it?" I asked, chuckling at my own joke. I didn't take him all the way to the top of the mountain, but we reached a plateau that formed a wonderful viewing platform. The world stretched out ahead of us. I placed my hand on Deke's shoulder and enjoyed sharing this special moment with my son.

"In the city there are so many people, Deke. You have to share it with all of them. There's no place you can call your own, but out here this is all yours. It's your birthright, just as it was my birthright. This land is beautiful, and it's all ours. But you know, it's better if you could see it from another vantage point. You know those dreams where you fly? Imagine if you were up there now," I pointed up to the sky and got him to follow my gaze. "You could be soaring among the clouds and looking down upon the desert, swooping close before rising again and looking at the pattern of the world. It would be amazing, wouldn't it?" I said.

Deke nodded.

"Would you like to fly, Deke?" I asked.

"Yes," he said.

I felt a swell of pride again. It was the right answer. He truly was my son and nothing Kira or anyone else could say would change that fact. I moved my hand from his shoulder to his back and knew that he was about to embrace his destiny. I closed my eyes, choosing to embrace the moment, before I pushed him towards his fate. I sent him hurtling towards the edge of the plateau and then watched as he was taken by gravity, waiting for that moment when he would spread his wings and become the dragon that I knew he could be.

Chapter Seventeen

Kira "It's all my fault. I knew I shouldn't have left him alone. I
knew I shouldn't have gone out to the lake. I'm his mother. I'm
supposed to protect him," I spat as I paced outside the ranch, kicking
up dirt as I walked back and forth. Anger and frustration boiled inside
me and all I wanted was to tear my hair out.

"It's not your fault, Kira. You have to be allowed to enjoy some time
by yourself," Gordy said. Of course he would say that. All he wanted
was for us to be boyfriend and girlfriend like he always wanted when
we were teenagers. Life has moved on though and it's not so simple.
Hell, I couldn't blame him entirely for that though. I felt the same
thing myself, before reality came crashing back. The truth is he's too
sentimental to realize that I'm bad news for him so I have to be the one
who makes sure he doesn't make a mistake.

"You don't know what it's like to be a parent," I said, perhaps too
harshly.

"If anyone is to blame then it's me. You put him under my care and
I let Tristan take him. I should have put up more of a fight," Rock said.

"No, Dad, you did what was right. The truth is I can't stop Tristan
from being around Deke. I just wish I was there so I could listen to the
things he's telling him."

"We have to find him," Gordy said.

"He could be anywhere," Dad moaned.

"No, not anywhere. He'll take Deke into the mountains. Tristan
always liked the mountains. It's just a matter of finding which one," I
said. I didn't think Deke was in danger. Tristan was many things, but
he never would have harmed his own son. I was more worried about

him telling Deke the truth. The last thing I wanted was for Tristan to undo all the hard work and all the sacrifices I had made. I pulled Gordy away and jumped in his truck again. Maybe it was too arrogant of me to think that he was automatically going to help me after what had just happened between us. I couldn't let myself get pushed into something I wasn't ready for though, and I knew that Gordy wanted more than I could promise. He always had. That's why I had gone for Tristan in the first place. Gordy was the kind of man you settled down with, and when I was younger I hadn't wanted to settle down at all.

I should have just kept kissing him by the lake instead of telling him to stop. It was easier to kiss him than to speak about things I didn't want to speak about. He was a good kisser too, which kind of surprised me actually. I never realized how passionate he had been.

I had to put that out of my mind for the time being though. Gordy's truck spat up a wave of dust as he turned and we surged across the desert in search of Tristan and Deke. Even with all the worry of the city I had never lost Deke like this before. There was a kind of panic that set in that made it feel as though the world was spinning erratically and I couldn't regain my footing.

"Tristan isn't going to hurt Deke," Gordy said, no doubt in an effort to quell my feelings.

"I know," I replied.

"I don't know what's gotten into him."

"I do. He just wants to be with his kid," I said. "To be honest I'm beginning to have doubts about whether I did the right thing in keeping Deke away from him. I took him to the city and disappeared. People change over five years. Maybe he is ready to be more of a father figure to Deke."

"Maybe, but he still should have asked you. He knew that you were away from the ranch. He chose that moment to get Deke. I'm not going to let him forget this. I'm not going to let him get away with this. He's taken it too far," Gordy said. I felt a flare of arousal at the way he spoke.

I had no qualms with fighting my own battles, but the fact that Gordy was willing to fight for me as well was intriguing. I still had no plans to stay here for any length of time though, so I wasn't about to let myself fall into the trap of getting too attached to Gordy.

The day was still bright and in the distance I saw the sun gleam against a truck that had been parked at the bottom of a mountain. I guided Gordy towards it. He pressed his foot down hard on the accelerator and the world became a blur. I never let my gaze drift from the mountain, and then I saw something that filled me with horror.

Gordy saw it too.

We both cursed.

He slammed the brakes and the truck almost flipped over. I was already climbing out the door. Gordy was half a second behind me. I wasted no time in spreading my wings. I was running at full pelt and then suddenly I was rising from the ground, pressing my wings flat to my back before creating a huge gust of momentum. I had always been the swiftest dragon and I could not afford my speed to fail me now, because my son was plummeting through the air, and if I didn't reach him in time he would crash to the ground and nothing would be left but a bloody smear.

I could feel Gordy behind me, trying to keep up, but he was going to be late. It was me or nothing.

Where the hell was Tristan?

I tried to gauge how far Deke had left to fall. I wasn't sure I was going to make it in time. My heart pounded. Thunder was in my ears. If anything happened to him... damn Tristan and damn this place and damn our dragon souls. I hurtled through the air, plummeting down against the side of the mountain, seeing my little boy falling, his limbs splayed out, his body so small and vulnerable. In my mind I could already hear the sickening crack of impact. I could already feel my heart breaking. But no, not yet. I still had a chance. There was still a chance. I surged forward. My stomach was almost scraping the ground.

At the last moment I spread open my wings and caught Deke before he crashed down. I ascended through the air, holding him close. His eyes were closed, his body limp, but he was still breathing. The terror of it all must have rendered him unconscious.

Anger blazed within my heart as I flew up the side of the mountain, darting towards the plateau where I could see Tristan standing, peeking over the cresting rocks. My eyes narrowed. I landed, slamming my feet onto the rocky surface. Tristan was still in his human form. I opened my scaly maw and let out a barrage of a scream. The hot air knocked him back, and I was just about ready to breathe fire as well, to burn Tristan into ash.

But I stopped myself from doing that.

There was a pact us dragons had to never do such a thing when another dragon was in a human form, but then again we should have had a pact to not kidnap children and push them off a mountain. My eyes twitched with rage and my claws were ready to tear Tristan apart, but somehow I managed to keep myself under control and shift back into my human form. I may not have been able to spit fire at him, but I could sure as hell spit venomous words. I lay Deke calmly on the ground and checked him over quickly to ensure that he was alright. Aside from being unconscious he seemed well enough. There were no marks or bruises on his body. I kissed his forehead, and thought to myself that it was a blessing in disguise that he was unconscious as I didn't have to explain that I could turn into a dragon. That could wait until later though. Right now I had Tristan to deal with.

I glared at him with fury and strode towards him, my arms rigid by my side. Now that I was no longer a dragon he had grown in confidence and began to speak. I wasn't going to bother listening to any words though. I walked right up to him and slapped him across the face, so hard that my palm stung. Tears glistened in my eyes and I trembled, so fervent was my anger.

"What the hell do you think you're doing? What are you doing with my son? Are you trying to kill him? I should throw you off that mountain myself, and I would, if I could tie your wings down. I've thought so many things about you over the years, Tristan, but I never thought you'd stoop this low. Is this the kind of man you've turned into? Are you really willing to kill your own child?" I spat, the words hot and hard as they shot out of my mouth. I grit my teeth and the emotion was so wild in me that I was ready to explode. Tristan kept his distance from me, taking a step backwards. My gaze never left him. I was ready to kill him, this man I had once loved, this man who had fathered my child.

Chapter Eighteen

Tristan

I had to hold my anger in check. Kira was angry enough for the both of us. I could see it radiating out of every pore. To see her as a dragon again though... what a sight that was. It was an amazing sight, a glory to behold. I couldn't believe she would give all that up for the sake of living in the city. I couldn't believe she would hide that most cherished part of her. It made me sick.

And then she dared accuse me of trying to kill my own child.

"I would never do such a thing! All I wanted was to spend time with him, to show him what he is truly capable of and I was so close! So close! But you had to come along and ruin it."

"Ruin it?!" she shrieked. "You think that saving my son is ruining anything? What the hell were you thinking, tossing him off a mountain? Are you insane? I started to believe that you were losing your mind, but I never believed how much you actually have changed. What could have possessed you to do this? What could have made you think any of this was a good idea?" Her voice was shrill and it echoed through the canyons like a thunderstorm.

Before I could answer her, Gordy appeared. His long body rose up and cast a shadow over us. His reptilian eyes gazed at us and took stock of the scene before him. When he saw that we were both in our human form he descended to the ground and shifted into his human form as well. It was better for him that he did. If we were both dragons I would have just defeated him in combat again. I snarled as Gordy came striding to Kira's side as if he belonged there, as though he had taken my place.

"What the hell are you thinking, Tristan?" he asked, echoing Kira's words. His voice boomed and anger was on his face. I don't know what right he thought he had to be here though. It wasn't as though he was coming to the defense of his child.

"I don't have to justify myself to you, Gordy. You have no business here," I said.

"I have every damn right to be here!" Gordy yelled back.

Before I could reply, Kira tugged his arm and spoke in a low voice, although not so low that I could not hear her words. She told him to leave, to take Deke back to Rock. I saw the concern flicker in Gordy's eyes. He did not want to leave her alone with me. I could sense the desire seeping out of every pore of his, and it sickened me. Hadn't he learned so long ago that she was mine? He turned away reluctantly and gathered Deke in his arms. Instead of flying down the mountain he walked, probably scared to be a dragon in case Deke woke up. I don't know what they were so scared of, or what they were trying to protect him from. Did they not have any faith in my son's strength? It was an insult. But I was glad to see Gordy leave either way. It was better that Kira and I have some time alone.

It had been too long, far too long.

"So? What do you have to say to explain yourself?" Kira asked, folding her arms across her chest. For a woman who could be so soft she looked incredibly hard in this moment, her body and face all sharp edges, her tongue lashing out with every word accompanied by a whipcrack in the air.

"I should think that was obvious. I only wanted to spend time with my son."

Kira barked a laugh and rolled her eyes. "You think this is some quality time? You think taking him to a mountain and pushing him off is the way to create a bond with him?"

"I think helping him to understand what he is will create a bond."

Her eyes narrowed. "I told you to leave it. I will tell him when I'm good and ready."

"That's not soon enough. He's ready now, Kira. You don't know what he's capable of."

"I know him a hell of a lot more than you do."

"Because you've kept him from me. Because you took him away."

"Because you told me to leave!" she yelled, throwing her arms up in the air.

"I didn't mean it!" I yelled too, the volume of my voice matching hers. "All you had to do was listen to me and believe me, but you kept acting as though I was crazy. I spoke in anger, and you were all too quick to heed my words. You couldn't get out of here quickly enough. Part of me wonders if you've ever wanted to be a dragon."

"Of course I wanted to be a dragon."

"Really? Because you gave it up pretty quickly and now you're trying to stop Deke from learning about his heritage. Is that what you're really trying to do? What happens when he starts feeling the urge? Are you going to tell him that there's some monster inside him? Are you going to carve his wings away and leave him a bloodied mess?"

"Of course not!" Kira said, although this time her words were ringed with sorrow. Her eyes glistened with tears. "But what are you going to do? Are you going to kill him?"

I slashed my arm through the air as though it was a hammer. "I was never going to kill him. I was only trying to wake the dragon in him."

"There isn't a dragon in him yet," Kira said.

"How do you know? Did he tell you he's been having dreams?"

She looked stunned and was knocked back a step. "Dreams?" she asked, her voice more of a whisper now.

"Yes, dreams. He told me. He's had dreams where he's flying through the air, soaring. He thinks he's a bird in his dreams, but the time will come soon where he learns the truth. The process has already begun, Kira. It's only a matter of time now before he learns to embrace the dragon within, and when that time comes there's no stopping it. You know that better than anyone. I mean, what were you thinking trying to keep this from him?"

"I was just trying to protect him. And throwing him off a cliff wasn't the right thing to do."

"If you had let him fall his instincts would have kicked in. He would have spread his wings and saved himself. The dragon in him wouldn't let him die."

"You don't know that. It was too much of a risk to take. If I hadn't been here..."

Her words faded into silence. I have to admit that I thought Deke would have shown his dragon sooner rather than falling through the air.

"I wasn't going to let him die," I mumbled. "I could have saved him."

"You should never have put him in that position in the first place," Kira said. "This is why I wanted to keep him away from here. It's too dangerous to be a dragon. He deserves a life of peace."

I scowled at her, unable to believe what I was hearing. "I can't believe you would deprive him of something so precious. This is who we are, Kira. This is who he is. It's his birthright and he deserves to know the truth. You keep telling me that I have no right to be his father, but are you sure that's the truth when I'm the only one who actually wants to be honest with him? If my only crime is wanting to tell my son that he's capable of being so much more than he is then I don't see it being that much of a crime. Can you really look me in the eye and tell me that I'm being unreasonable here? I've already missed out on five years of his life because you were so eager to run away from this place, and now he's back you expect me to just act like nothing happened? You expect me to act like he isn't my son? Have you really been gone that long that you've forgotten what kind of man I am?"

I leveled my gaze at her, waiting for her to respond. Five years seemed to melt away in an instant. I remember that last argument we had where she told me she was pregnant, and where I cursed her. I had been too harsh then. I hadn't realized all I had been giving up, but now that Deke was back in my life I wasn't ready to let her take him away from me again. He deserved to know the truth. He deserved to be my true son.

"I'm just trying to keep him safe," Kira said, softly this time.

"It's not going to work, Kira."

"Neither is your scheme to find Black Fang. He's a myth, Tristan. You can't conquer death. Nobody can. I won't let you fill Deke's head with these ideas either. Just stay away from him. Stay away from us. It'll be easier for everyone in the long run. I'm not going to stick around here, and I know how much you hate the city. You have your life and I have mine. Let's just leave it at that. We'll all be the better for it."

"And does Gordy know this as well? Or are you going to break his heart like you broke mine?"

Kira turned away, but showed me half of her face. "You broke my heart first. I don't want to hurt anyone. I never did. It's just that life has taken me on a different path than it has for you. I'm not going to pretend that it's easy. It's not. But I'm not going to put Deke in danger as well. I'll tell him about us in my own time, when I think he's ready. You can't force the issue, Tristan, and as much as you think you can be his father, you can't. I'm starting to think I should never have come back here."

The words may have sounded final, but I knew she was lying to herself because when she stepped away from the mountain she did not walk down the pass as a human would. Rather, she shifted into a dragon again and took to the skies, flying back to her father's ranch. I watched in awe, remembering why I had fallen in love with her in the first place. She might keep telling me to stay away from Deke, but that wasn't going to happen. He was my son and she was my mate, and while many things might change in the world, those two things remained constant.

It was just a matter of time until she saw that her place was with me, here, as a dragon.

Chapter Nineteen

G ordy

I carried Deke's limp body down and placed him in the passenger seat of my truck before driving back to the ranch, as Kira had instructed. I hated how she was up there alone with Tristan. He had that smug look on his face that I wanted to wipe away. Maybe a part of me was jealous as well considering the history they had. It was never more apparent than when I was standing there beside Deke, an interloper in this family feud. The kid was still unconscious. It had been a bold move by Tristan to try and force the boy to embrace the dragon, and it clearly hadn't worked. I smirked as I thought about the ranting anger that Kira would bestow upon Tristan as well. He was so used to living in his own world and getting his own way that he had forgotten what it was like to be told otherwise. Kira was such a spirited woman...

Damn.

I had no idea where I stood with her anymore. She seemed adamant that she was going to leave again. She could have a life here. I wanted to show her that she could have a life here, but where was I supposed to begin? What could I give her that nobody else could? Friendship didn't seem like it was going to be enough.

I pulled up outside Rock's ranch and got out. As soon as he heard the truck Rock was on the porch. Fear was written upon his face when he saw me carrying Deke in. Strength seeped from his knees and he had to support himself against the porch.

"Is he...?" Rock asked, unable to bring himself to utter the entire question.

"He's just unconscious. You might want to pour yourself a beer for this."

I HAD PLACED DEKE UPSTAIRS in his room and then returned downstairs. Rock had a beer ready for each of us. I took a long swig. I was thirstier than I realized.

"What the hell happened out there and where is my daughter?" Rock asked.

I explained everything as best I could and Rock cursed under his breath when he listened to my story.

"And she's still up there?" he asked. I nodded. "God knows what they're talking about," he ran a hand along his beard and looked every one of his years.

"She can take care of herself," I said.

"That's not what I'm worried about."

"What are you worried about?"

"Just this whole thing... the way her life has turned out. I remember when she was younger, how proud she was to be a dragon. But now she acts ashamed of it, as though this is something that she wants to cut out of her soul," Rock said.

"So you don't agree with her keeping the truth from Deke?"

He looked directly into my eyes and I could see the pain within them. "He's a dragon. As much as I disagree with Tristan on a lot of things, I think he's right about this. At some point it's going to become obvious. There's no denying it. We can't stop being dragons more than we stop breathing, and Kira is only going to make it harder for the boy. Not that I'd ever tell her that," he added the last part with a dry chuckle. "She has her way of doing things."

"I just wish I knew what to say around her. I say something and then she takes it in the wrong way and I have no idea what I'm supposed to do. One minute I think she's getting used to the idea of staying here, and the next she's talking about heading back to the city. I just don't know what I'm supposed to do. I want to be a good friend, but she doesn't make it easy."

"You think that's hard? Try being her father," Rock chuckled again, although his laughter turned into a hacking cough. He held a handkerchief to his mouth and when he took it away I saw that it was covered in dark phlegm. Through all this it had been easy to forget the man was suffering. He had always been such a vital, vigorous man and it was difficult to see him as sickly and wan. Maybe that had been playing on Kira's mind as well. Maybe there were just too many reminders of pain in this place for her to cope with.

It was a little while later when Kira returned. She wasn't in a truck, so I assumed that she had been in her dragon form. It warmed my heart to know that she was enjoying being a dragon again after forcing that part of herself aside for so long. But it did make me wonder how she could possibly return to the city and stop being herself. I had considered the possibility of returning to the city with her, if she would have me, but if I did that I would have to give up being a dragon. It came as naturally to me as breathing and I just couldn't imagine not being able to shift whenever I wanted. Perhaps in a way Kira was right. Was I just falling in love with the memory of her?

I stood in the doorway as she walked up the porch.

"How's Deke?" she asked, her words as blunt as ever.

"He's fine. I put him in his bed. What happened up there?"

"I don't want to talk about it."

"Kira..."

"I said I don't want to talk about it," she repeated, glaring at me as she waited for me to move aside. I stepped back, allowing her to come into the house. As soon as she was inside Rock came up to her and hugged her. Kira looked as though she was about to squirm though.

"I'm so sorry for what happened before. I should have tried harder to fight him off, it was just that he told Deke before I could do anything and I didn't think it would be good for the boy to see his father being thrown out of the house."

"Well, we won't have that problem any longer. I just told Tristan that I don't want anything to do with him, and I don't want him to have anything to do with Deke. He crossed the line today and I'm not going to have him fill Deke's head with things that he doesn't need to know about. This needs to stop right here. Deke is my child and I'll raise him as I see fit. There's no need for him to know about something that's going to hurt him."

She went into the kitchen to pour herself a drink. While she did this I glanced at Rock uneasily. When she came back into the lounge she noticed there was an awkward tension between us.

"What's going on?" she asked.

Her gaze passed between myself and Rock. I shrugged, and gestured for him to continue. He was her father after all.

"Are you sure you're going about this the right way? He is a dragon, after all. It's in his blood. You can't stop him from learning about it, and you can't stop him from growing wings. I'm not saying that Tristan was right to do what he did, but don't you think that Deke does deserve to know about his heritage?"

Rock's words were surprisingly soft, but the look on Kira's face was anything but. Shadows were under her eyes and her irises seemed to glow. It was impossible for us to breathe fire while in our human forms, but with her it seemed possible.

"And do you feel the same way?" she asked in a shrill voice, her head turning towards me. Only proximity had roped me into this conversation and I wished I could have made a hasty exit. I didn't know if I should be honest or if I should just tell her what she wanted to hear. In the end I opted for the former.

"I think it would make his life easier if he knew, yes," I said, and immediately realized that I had probably just killed my chances of being romantically involved with her. Although considering she had pulled away from me in a dramatic fashion I wasn't sure how good my chances with her were anyway.

"Right, well, I'm glad that all you men have a good idea of how to raise my son despite not being involved in his life for five years. If you don't mind I'm going to see him now, and I don't want to talk about this anymore either. He's my son and I'll raise him as I see fit," she said, and with that she turned and marched upstairs. I felt my heart sink and I wished things had gone differently, but I couldn't ignore the fact that she was making a mistake here. Deke was a dragon, and at some point he was going to find out for himself. It was better to do that here rather than in the city where there were people who would want to hunt and hurt him.

Chapter Twenty

K ira
Anger thrummed through my body as I marched upstairs, leaving Dad and Gordy behind. I couldn't believe the gall of them to side with Tristan. Why did everyone seem to think that how I raised Deke was any business of theirs? They were all so consumed with this idea of being a dragon, as though that was the only thing that made us matter in the world. I knew it was going to be a hard life for Deke, but there were other things that made us special, that made him special.

I went into his room and sat on the edge of his bed. I brushed a few strands of hair away from his face and kissed him on the forehead, waiting for him to stir. I thought about my conversation with Tristan and how he was so good at getting under my skin after all these years. There was a part of him that still resonated with me, and I hated myself for it. I hated myself for the way I had spoken to Gordy as well. He was too nice for this world, too nice for me as well. I had always suspected he had feelings for me, even back then, but he didn't have that hard edge to him like Tristan did. Gordy was the kind of man I should have fallen for, but it was probably too late now. My life was such a mess it was better for me to be on my own. I didn't fit into the human world, but I didn't fit into the dragon world either. I was just caught between the two, being pulled in either direction, and I was just hating the day when Deke would be forced to choose as well. I was so afraid he would choose a world without me in it, just like I had done when I had run away.

But that was something to be far in the future. Right now Deke was still just a child with a whole life to live yet. I caressed his cheek and kissed him softly again. This time he did stir. His eyes opened slowly, and he smiled at me.

"Mommy?" he asked with half a yawn.

"Hey Deke, yes it's me."

"What happened? I was with Dad," he said, the words coming out of his mouth slowly.

My throat tightened and I had to swallow down the bilious anger that festered there. "I know, do you remember what happened?"

He scrunched up his face as he tried to think. "I don't really. We were standing on the mountains and he was telling me how beautiful the world was and then I remember falling... I must have tripped I suppose," he said.

As much as I wanted to show him the kind of man his father was, I wasn't about to tell him that Tristan had pushed him off the mountain because Deke would only want to know why he had done such a thing, and that would mean revealing the truth.

"You're okay now though, Deke."

"But how?" he asked.

"There was a platform below where you fell. You didn't fall far at all. It's okay now. You're safe."

Deke nodded, thankfully accepting my explanation without any question. "Mommy, is that man really my Daddy?" he asked.

It was a question I had been dreading, but I suppose there was no use denying the truth any longer. "Yes, he is, Deke. I'm sorry that I didn't tell you before."

"Are you married?"

"No, Deke, we're not married. We're not together at all. We were, a long time ago, but then things changed and I went to live in the city with you."

"He said that he was sorry. He said that he missed me. He told me that we were going to spend lots of time together now that I'm back here."

My heart winced at this. It was the last thing I wanted Deke to say.

"Is that something you'd like to do?" I asked, praying that he gave the answer I wanted to hear. Instead, Deke shrugged and nodded.

"I guess so," he said.

"Well, I'm sure that's something we can arrange at some point," I said, hoping to delay it indefinitely, "but for the time being I think it's better that we stick to it being just you, me and Grandpa, okay? I know it must have been fun to spend time with him, but there's a lot of things you don't know about your Dad and... and we'll just think about," I said, tucking the sheets around him. While he had been hurt he had been out in the sun a lot and had clearly done a lot of walking. His head lolled to the side and his eyelids grew heavy as he started to slip into slumber.

"He asked me about my dreams," Deke said sleepily. "When I'm flying." I swallowed a lump in my throat as he referred to his dreams, to the part of him that I tried so hard to deny. Being a dragon was complicated and all I wanted to do was save him from the trouble that I had been through, but if the dreams had started then Tristan was right. It was only a matter of time before he developed more signs. I was on a ticking clock and I couldn't fight against it forever.

I left him to sleep, to be at peace for a time because I didn't know how long this peace could last.

I WALKED DOWNSTAIRS to find Rock and Gordy still sitting in the lounge. They stared at me as I approached. I sighed, knowing that I wasn't going to be able to avoid talking about these things.

"Gordy, do you mind coming up to my room?" I shouted down. Gordy rose and followed me back up the stairs. I walked into the room and paced beside the window. Gordy perched on the edge of the bed. I gnawed my lower lip and faced the window.

"I'm sorry for earlier. I'm sorry for everything. I know you haven't asked to be treated this way."

"You don't have to apologize," he said.

I closed my eyes. "Gordy, you don't always have to be the good guy. You can tell me when I'm being a jerk."

"It's not in my nature. Besides, I know that you've had a hard time of it. I know what you've been through. I don't have a kid. I don't know what it's like. All I want you to know is that I'm here for you and I'll do whatever you need for as long as you're here. I think I've wasted too much time in not being honest with myself and the people around me."

"I appreciate your honesty, I think. Do you really think I'm making a mistake with Deke?" I asked, my voice cracking. It had been so long since I had been able to ask anyone else for advice.

"I do," Gordy said. It must have taken him a lot of courage to say that because he was always the kind of boy who never wanted to upset people. I was glad to see him becoming a man. "It's not fair to keep the truth from him, Kira. He's only going to resent you for it when it comes time to tell him the truth. You can't stop him from being who he is, whether you like it or not, and I think you've spent too long denying the dragon inside you. I've seen what you're like when you embrace the dragon again. I can feel your excitement and the way you come alive and I'm guessing you haven't felt like that since you left. Maybe being a dragon isn't as bad as you remember."

"I'm just so worried about him," I said, my head dipping. I placed it in my hands and felt a hot stream of tears burning my hands. "He told me he's started dreaming. It's going to happen and there's nothing I can do to stop it."

"Maybe you don't need to stop it. Maybe you just need to be around people who can give him support and advice. Kira, the city isn't the right place for you or him. He needs to be with his own kind. I think that maybe you do as well. You said it yourself; you're so lonely out there. What kind of life is that to live? You want the best life for

Deke, but I'm sure that he wants the best life for you as well. And I have to say that I'm lonely without you as well. Since you've come back I realize what's been missing from my life," he said, getting up from the bed. I heard his footsteps against the floor as he came towards me, then suddenly his hands were upon my waist and he was standing behind me. My skin tingled with excitement as I felt his breath against the nape of my neck. I could have pulled away from him, but I didn't.

I turned to look him in the eyes. I had fought against so many things, but I was tired of fighting. I just wanted to feel something good again, something other than fear or bitterness or loneliness. And I think Gordy was the same. We were bringing out the best in each other and as he took me into his arms I melted into the kiss again, knowing that with every moment it lasted I was bringing myself back into the home of dragons.

Chapter Twenty One

G ordy

She was so soft, so beautiful. When I kissed her I felt as though we were soaring through the air. My heart was lighter than it had ever been before and I knew true happiness. Our mouths parted and I gazed into her liquid eyes, feeling the heat from her tongue lingering on my lips. It was glorious, and it made my soul shake. Excitement danced in her eyes and I could feel that something was happening. She turned away from me and opened the window up. She placed her hands against the window sill and gazed out into the quiet and calm night.

"I feel like I want something to happen tonight, Gordy. I know that my life is never going to be the same. I'm going to have to talk to Deke about this, but while he's sleeping I want to do something for myself. I want to..." she trailed away and for a moment I wondered what was on her mind. Kira had always been the unpredictable kind. I guess that was part of what made her so intoxicating. Then she jumped out of the window. I raced to the window and looked out, a flare of worry rising inside me, but I shouldn't have worried at all. I saw a beautiful dragon ascending from the ground, wings spread, tail flicking, looking majestic as she was framed by the stars. She turned her head towards me and there was something coy about her beady eyes, beckoning me to follow her. I smirked as I climbed out of the window myself and shifted in mid air, embracing the dragon within me as she raced off, darting across the desert. I flapped my wings and tried my best to keep up with her, pushing myself to my limits. I was only able to keep her in my sight because she allowed me, but there was something comforting in knowing that she wanted me to catch her.

We raced through the night, making a path through the mountains, twisting and winding. Sometimes I saw her entire lithe body, whereas other times I only had the flick of a tail to guide me. Then I saw her moving towards the lake. It was hard to not just stand there and appreciate the sight of her as a dragon again. She had always been the most beautiful of us whether in human or dragon form, and I could feel my wasted heart falling in love with her all over again. It was a wretched, pathetic thing, but I could not help myself. Kira had always been elusive and I knew full well that she might well end up wanting to leave again, but even if I could only be with her for one night... what a night it would be.

I followed her to the lake and saw her glide down into the still water, the deep lake engulfing her long mythical body. The ripples faded and by the time I grew close enough to see properly she rose from the water, a human head appearing, her hair lank against her scalp and shoulders, her milky skin pale in the cool water. I gently descended down. My tail pierced the surface of the water and as I submerged I shifted back as well, returning to my human form. I shivered a little. The water was a great deal cooler than it had been in the daytime. There was a lump in my throat as I swam towards her, closing the distance between us. The night was dark but the moon was bright, casting us in silver light. She looked ethereal and so beautiful as the light framed her in this wondrous, glittering illumination. The water bobbed towards the hollow of her throat. Tension gripped me. Beyond this water she was naked. Suddenly heat began to spread through my body and I was not cold any longer.

"How many times did you used to think about being in the lake with me when we were younger, Gordy?" she asked, her voice as soft as the water around us.

I was almost embarrassed to answer the question. "Probably too many times," I admitted. It brought a wide smile to her face.

"I think I should have come with you here a long time ago. I've been thinking a lot about what's happening to me and I've begun to realize that I tend to deny myself too many things. You're a good man, Gordy, and you've only ever wanted the best for me. Even now when I've been so cruel to you, you still stand by me and are ready to offer advice and support. I know I'm not the perfect girl, but I think I've gained enough wisdom over the years to be able to know that I shouldn't turn away from you again."

She moved towards me, closing the distance between us even more. The water rippled gently in reaction to her movements. Our legs danced under the water, keeping us afloat. Beneath the veil of liquid I felt one of her hands take mine. It was something solid amid the gentle, lilting water. Her other hand pressed against my body, laying flat against my torso. That taut knot deep in my stomach tightened again and I thought my heart was going to burst out of my chest. My lips parted as my arms wrapped around her, cradling her soft body, holding her against me. Our heat burned and I was surprised the water did not begin to hiss and boil. I brushed some strands of wet hair away from her face, while my other hand rested against the curve of her hip. The water shimmered, depriving me of seeing her naked beauty. Somehow that aroused me even more; the tension and the excitement building up inside me. I kissed her again, feeling everything unspool within me. I felt the fire on her lips and the eagerness of her tongue and I knew for one night, at least, she would be mine. My hands ran around her back and felt the wetness of her hair draped over them. I felt the rhythm of her breathing, her breasts pressed against my chest, my arousal a hard anchor pulsing in the lake.

Her hand dropped down. She smiled and let out a long exhalation as she gripped it. I moaned, a low and terse sound that was more like a bestial growl as our kiss deepened. I wanted her more than I had wanted anything else in the world. All the years of longing, all the near misses, were finally being redeemed and something was being unlocked inside me. We swam through the waves and it was as though we were flying through the air. Our bodies were entwined to the point where it was impossible to tell where one of us ended and the other began. Our legs were locked together, our arms curled around each and held each other tightly, while our lips were pressed against each other, drinking in sweet kisses over and over again. We made our way to the edge of the lake where the ground was shallower underneath.

I lay against the bank, my chest showed. Crystal water dripped down my broad muscles, making the hair on my chest seem darker. She remained a little distance away, still wanting to tease me, to make me wait, to take me to the breaking point until I could finally see her in all her glory. She moved forward, the water falling away like a dress, revealing her body inch by inch. My mouth dropped open as I saw her flawless, milky skin being exposed. The swelling curves of her body, so feminine and so alluring made my heart quake. Her nipples were pink and already hard, and my eyes immediately fell to her hourglass hips and the dark shadow in between her thighs. A deep hunger swelled within me and I moved forward, catching her in my arms. She shrieked with delight as I pulled her towards me, and I knelt at her feet, wanting to worship her. Water sloshed against my neck as I looked up at her, hoping that she knew how long I had wanted this, how badly I needed this, and then I leaned forward and breathed in the sweetness of her womanly essence.

Warmth ran over my tongue as I kissed her and teased her, burying myself against her. I curled my arms around her back as she tilted her head back, moaning into the open air as burning arousal surged through our bodies. I lovingly caressed her with my tongue, enjoying the tremors that shuddered through her as she stood before me, a goddess made flesh. My fingers sank into her supple skin and when I looked up at her I saw her voluptuous breasts rise with every heaving breath and I witnessed the pleasure dancing upon her face. She was the personification of beauty, in every sense of the word, and my mind was cast in a hazy dream. Part of me thought I was going to wake as I didn't believe this could actually be real, but she was there. I was tasting her. The sweet musk trickled down the back of my throat and I gorged on her for more, bringing her closer and closer to the sweet tension that eventually curdled inside her and came out in a warm stream, drenching my lips and dazzling my tongue. I leaned back, gasping in breath, gazing up at her with desire and yearning. I hoped she would be able to see it in my eyes; this thing I had inside my heart. I wanted so badly for her to stay.

She placed her hands upon my shoulders and gently pushed me back to the bank. Water spread around my body and left us in strong ripples. I sat on the bank, the water around my mid section. She fell and crawled towards me, her body submerged in the water again. It drifted around her curves, occasionally giving me a glimpse of her naked wonder. I reached out to caress her, but she pushed my hand away, instead reaching under the water and clasping her hands around my manhood. She guided me up and the water fell away, revealing my hard arousal. She looked at me through hooded eyes as she lowered her head and took me into her mouth. She teased me at first, because of course she was going to tease me. Her tongue flicked out to lash at my sensitive tip while her lips came together in a sweet kiss. She began to massage the taut skin before opening her mouth wider and taking more of me. My head arched back as the pleasure lanced through me like a bolt of fire. My breaths deepened and the storm inside me was a hell of a contrast compared to the stillness of the lake and the quietness of the night. My fingers gripped the hard dirt and the rock as she took me closer and closer to the pulsing sweetness that had eluded me for so long. My grip was so hard I thought I was going to break the rock off entirely. Desire throbbed within my head and careened around my body. Her lips were soft, and as she moved her head back and forth the water rippled around me, adding another layer to the sensations.

At one point she drew her head back and I moaned in anguish, thinking it was sheer torture that she would stop now when I was so close to paradise. But she swam in between my legs, adjusting her body so that her top half was out of the water. Her breasts shone as they were doused in water, capturing the moonlight as it fell from the heavens. Her head was tilted to the side and her eyes were wide. I had never seen anyone so beautiful. I leaned forward, reaching out, pulling her towards me. I dragged her from the water and kissed her again, this time enjoying her wet body as she fell against me. Her hair framed our faces like a veil and our hot breath swirled together. My hands fell against her hip again and I could feel her simmering arousal calling to me. She shifted her body with a coy smirk and I arched my head back, feeling the burst of pleasure as she pressed herself against me. She reached down and then suddenly our bodies were as one. The sheer exhilaration of the sensation was enough to make my body rock and send another strong series of waves rippling across the lake.

Kira leaned back herself, placing her palms against my chest to support herself as I got to witness her in all her glory. Droplets of water continued to spill from her flesh. I reached up, playing with her ample breasts and teasing her hard nipples. I ran a hand up to her mouth and watched her suck on my finger as she rode me, twisting and angling her body in such a way as to send me wild with desire. Her hair fell across her face and we never broke eye contact. Her eyes sparkled as brightly as the stars and I brought her to me again, kissing her, wanting to hold her tightly as if to tell her that I never wanted to let her go. The fire burned deeply within us. Our moans drifted together in the air, dancing as passionately and fiercely as our bodies. Our souls were alive, as were our hearts, and the song that was in our blood was a passionate, vibrant symphony that reached a glorious crescendo when it all quaked and tremored through me. I gripped her tightly as I howled and broke the silence of the night. The torrent of orgasm poured through me and erupted like a volcano. For a moment everything was pulsing and blinking, before suddenly fading to the quiet stillness of the night once again.

We lay against the bank of the lake. I idly traced my fingers along her back, twirling her thick, heavy locks of hair. Kira's head lay against my chest. She seemed to enjoy the furious beating of my heart. I lay back and gazed up at the stars. It felt like the perfect night. It felt as though, for the first time in my life, that nothing could go wrong.

"That was..." I began, but found that I could not find adequate words to encapsulate the way I felt about what we had just experienced together.

"It sure was," she replied, kissing my chest lightly, punctuating her words with a soft laugh. There was no way to hide from my feelings now, and I knew that if I wasn't honest with her I risked losing her. I ran a hand across her face and tilted it towards me so that I could look directly into her eyes.

"Don't leave again," I said, finally saying the things I wished I had said when she went away the first time. She licked her lips. There was a trace of a smile upon her face.

"I'm not going to," she said, and my heart leapt for joy. However, she had not finished speaking. "I need to talk to Deke though, about who he is. I just hope he doesn't hate me for hiding it from him."

"He won't. He might be angry for a while, but you're his Mom. You've taken care of him his entire life. There's no way he's going to want to lose that."

Kira looked uncertain, but I had absolutely no doubt about it. "There's something as well though; if I'm going to stay here then I'm going to have to find a way to make this work with Tristan. Eventually, Deke is going to want to spend time with his father, and it's only fair that he should, I suppose."

"It's not going to be easy, but I'll be by your side every step of the way," I said.

"Thanks, Gordy," she added a kiss to her words. I wanted so badly to tell her that I loved her, but something told me she wasn't ready for that. I kept the feeling locked inside me for a while longer, knowing that I would do anything to be with her. Now that I had gotten closer to her and fully embraced the feelings that had always been within me I knew that I could not live without her. I continued to hold her in my arms, wishing the night was endless, but also looking forward to everything the world promised us.

Chapter Twenty Two

Tristan

There was no way Kira was going to keep me from seeing my son, no matter what she thought of my plans. It was downright negligent to keep him from learning about his heritage. Yes, I may have been a little dramatic with my stunt earlier, but I truly thought Deke would spread his wings and fly. I realized I was going to need to find some other way to bring out the dragon in him. It was only a matter of time before it showed itself, but I was going to have to do it without Kira knowing about it. Damn her... she had once been so perfect. I thought we were going to usher in a new era for dragons together with her as my mate, but she had left and turned her back on me, and she had stolen my son as well.

Now it was my turn to raise him.

I was so close to finding Black Fang and I saw Deke as a sign that we could do it together. What better way to gain immortality than to have a father and son finding the legendary dragon together? And if there was anyone who could help Deke find his true nature it would be Black Fang himself.

I watched and waited until I saw Gordy and Kira fly off in the distance, leaving Deke alone with Rock. The night was long and dark. I flew to Rock's ranch in my dragon form and hovered outside the window. The old man was out cold, his head arched back with heavy snores coming out of his mouth. I moved to Deke's window. The child was wrapped in a blanket, sleeping soundly. My eyes narrowed with anger at the thought that he was being deprived of his legacy. A clawed hand moved to the window. It had been left open a crack, allowing the cool air of the night to drift in. I pushed it open and shifted into my human form as I climbed in the window, kneeling by his bed and shaking him awake.

It took Deke a few moments to stir. He gazed at me through sleepy eyes.

"Hey Deke, it's your Daddy," I whispered. He rubbed his eyes and sat up, confused.

"Where's Mommy?" he asked.

"Mommy is sleeping," I said, knowing there wasn't any point in wasting time. "You remember what we were talking about earlier? How we could stop people from being sick? Well I think I've found the thing that can help us. I'd like you to come with me so we can find it together. And I think I can help you with your dreams as well."

"I should ask Mommy," he said, turning towards the door. I clenched my jaw with frustration.

"You don't need to ask her Deke. I'm your Daddy. I'm not going to let anything happen to you," I said, trying to sound as calm as possible. "Look, there's something about you that you need to know, about all of us really. It's a secret we share that your Mommy hasn't told you about yet, and it has to do with your dreams. I can tell you what it is, but I need you to come with me, okay?" I said, holding out my hands. He gazed at them for what was an interminably long time, before taking them. My heart rejoiced as I took him from his bed and got him dressed in more suitable attire. I didn't want him to think we were doing anything untoward, so we left via the door rather than the window. I was afraid that Rock would wake or that Kira would choose this unfortunate moment to return and disrupt my plans, but neither fear came to pass. It gave me more confidence that this had been ordained, that this was destiny.

WE LEFT THE RANCH. Deke was still holding my hand. He was so small compared to me and as I looked at him it did give me a sense of pride to know that he wouldn't have been in this world if it had not been for me, and Kira, I suppose. The more I looked at him the more I saw some of her influence and I suppose I should have been grateful to her for raising my child to be such a well behaved boy. It did make me think of the times we had shared together, how she had intoxicated me with her beauty and twisted my soul into a new shape. It had been difficult to live without her these past five years. I hadn't truly realized how difficult it had been until she returned, or how much her love had been a part of my life. When she left she had ripped it away without a second thought. As much as she blamed me for things she had hurt me too, and she had taken my son with her. Well, now that he was in my life I was not going to let him be taken away again. If she tried she was going to have a hell of a fight.

"Are we going to walk to the mountains?" Deke asked. I could feel the worry in his voice as the mountains were some distance away.

I smirked. "That would take a long time, more than a day and a night. No, I have a better way of going about things," I said. "But it means I have to tell you this secret we share. It might be difficult to understand at first, but you're a brave boy, aren't you?" I asked. Deke nodded enthusiastically. "I thought so. Well, it's to do with your dreams. You said that you dream about flying, and you think it's something to do with a bird, but it's not. Do you know of any other creature that flies?"

Deke had a thoughtful look on his face as he considered the question, but then shook his head.

"What about dragons?" I asked.

"Dragons aren't real. They're just from stories," he replied.

I chuckled. "Oh they're very real, Deke, and you're one of them. So am I, and so is Mommy."

Deke stopped walking and looked at me with confusion etched upon his face. I leaned on my haunches so that I could make level eye contact with him. I kept hold of his hand as well. "I know this is difficult to understand, but there are lots of different types of people in the world. Some of us can change into dragons. That's why you've been having the dreams you've been having. It means that one day you're going to change into a dragon too."

"I don't want to change," Deke said, fear filling his eyes.

"Oh, but you will. Being a dragon is the best thing there is. It means we can fly, and we can breathe fire, and we can be so strong. Nothing can be stronger than us, Deke. It's the most wonderful feeling there is. And it means that you'll just be like Mommy and Daddy."

He considered this for a moment and then replied. "But Mommy has never been a dragon."

"I know," I sighed, "but that's because it's been dangerous for her in the city. But out here we can be dragons as often as we like, and that's how we're going to get to the mountains. We're going to fly. Would you like to fly, Deke?" I asked, already knowing that he would say yes. I loved his spirit of adventure, although it was bittersweet knowing it was something he had inherited from his mother.

"I want you to try something for me, Deke. I want you to think really hard about flying, so hard that you can imagine yourself flying as well, and if you feel something starting to rise inside you I want you to embrace it," I said. Deke clamped his eyes shut and began to think, but he did not change into a dragon. It was still not yet time for him. I reassured him it was okay and then I asked him if he would like to see me turn into a dragon. I promised that I wasn't going to hurt him and that he had nothing to be scared of, although I hoped that since he had the blood of dragons in him the sight of one would not fill him with fear.

I then stood tall in front of my son and held out my arms, remembering when my own father had done the same thing for me. I wondered if Deke would feel the same awe and the same immense power that I had felt in that moment. I embraced the dragon and grew in height, and when I opened my eyes again I was gazing down at my son.

I swelled with pride when I realized he wasn't looking at me with any fear. I lay flat on the ground, making myself as low as possible and gestured with my wings for him to climb onto my back. He mounted me and gripped my scales tightly. I spread my wings and began to soar into the sky, moving at a slower pace than usual as I wanted to allow Deke to get used to the sensation. I craned my head back and out of a beady eye I could see his mouth open in wonder, and I knew that soon he would be flying alongside me as my son, and there was nothing Kira could do to change it now.

But first we had to go and find Black Fang and change the lives of the dragons for the better.

WE FLEW FAR AND WIDE across the mountains. I had scoured these lands in search of Black Fang so often over the last five years, and had managed to narrow down where I thought he had made his lair. It was in an old mountain that had likely once been a volcano. I had a feeling that Black Fang was old enough to remember the volcano when it was erupting with the force of life. He must have seen so many things over the years. How the world would have changed under his watchful eye. Envy burned in my heart as I thought about the wonder of being able to see the world evolve and grow rather than having to pass on under the shroud of death and be forever in the dark about what happened in the world during your absence.

I reached the mountain and landed, allowing Deke to climb off my back before I shifted back into my human form. The rock was brittle and shadows seemed to come alive. Deke moved closer to me, hugging my legs because he was afraid.

"There's nothing to be scared of here, Deke, we're just here to see a very old dragon who is going to help us save those who are sick. Once we see him we can go back to your grandfather and make sure that he never gets sick again," I said. Deke calmed down, although in truth, I wasn't completely sure about what was going to happen once I found Black Fang. Despite all my research I had never been able to define how he had managed to become immortal. Such a thing must have cost a hefty price, which was probably why no other dragons pursued the same goal as Black Fang. We were kindred spirits, visionaries who were not respected by our peers. I hoped Black Fang would appreciate my tribute to him. He must have been waiting so long for someone to piece together the mystery and come and find him. I wondered if he grew lonely or frustrated at the passage of time, but I suppose that when you had all the time in the world the days would just blend into each other, as would the years, and they would not end up meaning much at all.

I had brought a flashlight with me and switched it on. The beam of light fought back against the shadows as we walked deeper into the caves. Deke gasped occasionally at the hint of movement, but there wasn't anything around us. We walked through a narrow passage and had to inch along a ravine. It would have been easier if Deke was able to turn into a dragon, but we would manage nevertheless. We entered a cave with huge stalactites descending from the ceiling, resembling spears that were just waiting to fall. The innards of this mountain felt like an abandoned world, one that was lost to time. It was fascinating and incredible, although Deke just seemed to think it was eerie. He shuddered and in his small, reedy voice he told me again that he was scared.

"I want to go home. I want to see Mommy," he whined.

"We'll see Mommy again soon, and you can make her happy by saying that you've found a way to save your grandfather. We won't be long, Deke, I promise. Nothing is going to hurt you here. I'm not going to let anything hurt you. We're just going to find Black Fang and he's going to teach us the secrets of how to save people. Nobody we love is ever going to have to get sick and die," I said, patting him on the back in the hope of reassuring him. I wasn't sure it worked, so I tightened my grip on his hand and forced him to march through the caverns of the mountain in case he was tempted to turn tail and flee.

I wasn't sure how long we had been walking for before we reached the bowels of the volcano, a huge cavern that stretching up into the darkness, preventing me from seeing the ceiling. I gasped, for the walls were shining with jewels that had been embedded into the rock. There was another huge pile of jewels and coins as well, and from somewhere the sound of trickling water greeted my ears. But these weren't the things that caught my attention the most. No, for what lay along the jewels on a wide plateau was a huge black dragon, bigger than any other dragon I had seen before. Its scales were as brittle as rock, its tail long and wicked. There was a haggard appearance as well, with scars and other flecked marks running along the scales, as if to show that this dragon had weathered a great deal of trauma. Its eyes were golden and I was filled with a sense of awe as it turned its head to look upon us. It reared up, and my mouth dropped even lower at the sheer size of him. Its neck was as thick as a mountain. Its wings were draped along its flank, so formidable. I was so overwhelmed I dropped to my knees.

The dragon peered at us and opened its mouth. I saw the Black Fang, charred by the strength of its own flame. It was him, the one I had been searching for all my life. Tears glistened in my eyes. People had always told me I was a fool, that it had only been an illusion. But I had known what I had seen and now he was there before me again, the proof that I was not a madman, the proof that I had been vindicated.

And then Black Fang spoke.

"Who dares disturb my slumber," he said. His voice was cracked and ancient, and it rumbled around the cavern like thunder. I had never known a dragon to be able to talk like a human while in dragon form before, and I sensed it must have been an ability that Black Fang had learned after years of being alive. My mind leaped with excitement at the thought of what else we were capable of.

"Your humble servant," I said in a shaking voice. "My name is Tristan, and this is my son, Deke. We are dragons too. A long time ago, when I was a child, I saw you. I searched your name and became fascinated with your story. People told me it was just a tale and there was no truth to it, but I knew differently. Now I have found you. I come in seek of knowledge. I come to seek the ability to live forever."

Black Fang studied us closely and a noise that resembled a laugh emerged from its throat, although it sounded more like rock being hammered away.

"Ah yes, a fellow dragon. How is the thunder doing? I have observed them from time to time, wondering if they are ever going to break away from their foolish thinking."

"They have not. They still cling to their old ways. But I want to show them there is another way. I want to teach them what you have learned," I said.

"It was the same in my day. People were not willing to make the sacrifice to ensure their immortality. Are you willing to do what must be done?" Black Fang asked.

"I am," I replied, my heart thundering in my chest. Black Fang's mouth twisted in a serpent's smile.

"Good, good, although I am offended that you come to my realm in that form," he spat.

"It is an old habit. I... I was not sure if it was true that you shed your human form," I muttered, not wishing to get into how I had only been in this form to make it easier for Deke to cope with the journey.

"Human flesh is weak. It can be torn apart easily. Not like dragon scales. To be immortal you must embrace the dragon. Forever," Black Fang said. Each word was monstrous and laden with ancient wisdom. I was ready to place myself before him, to do whatever he asked if it meant I could learn everything he had to teach.

"Yes... yes I am ready. I will do as you ask. I am ready to make the sacrifice, to surrender the ability to shift in order to gain eternal life and never be vulnerable to the weakness of disease or old age," I said.

Black Fang laughed again. I wasn't entirely sure what was so funny. Deke remained beside me. I don't think he fully understood what was going on. I would have to explain it to him later. I hadn't expected things to move this swiftly. I was going to have to leave my human form behind. I hoped there would be a way for me to still be Deke's father. I had just gotten used to spending time with him, but this was an opportunity I could not pass up on. I bowed my head, awaiting Black Fang's wisdom.

"That was not the sacrifice I meant," he said as he spread his wings. One flap was enough to send a strong gust of air towards us. Deke held onto me tightly. "The others were too weak to do what needed to be done. Immortal life needs the blood of another. The blood of the young. The blood of your child," Black Fang said.

Color drained from my cheeks. My eyes went wide and my throat went dry. Confusion was a miasma in my mind. How could this be? How could it require something so evil?

Then it twigged in my mind. I had never truly explored the reason why the other dragons had not followed Black Fang's lead. I had always thought it was simply because they were too attached to their human lives and had not wanted to shed their mortal flesh. I had never wondered if there was more to the story... but of course there was. Black Fang must have asked his peers to do something so horrible they had no choice but to shun him and exile him. He must have murdered his own children in order to gain immortal life and that is why the story had been passed down from generation to generation as a grim warning to anyone who let themselves be blinded by ambition and greed.

"You have already made the first step by bringing him here. Now take the boy's life and you can join me. For so long I have waited for an equal, for another dragon to be my companion. Join me and together we can wreak havoc across the skies. We can burn the heavens and tear the world asunder. There will be nothing we cannot accomplish. All it takes is one act of courage. Embrace your true self, dragon, and let me see your son's blood stain the rocks of my home."

His words were chilling. I turned to Deke as tears filled my eyes. Is this how it was all going to end? I knew our destinies had been bound together, but I had never wanted it to end like this. I tried to quell the beating of my heart and I tried to force away the lump that had appeared in my throat. I looked into Deke's eyes. It was clear that he did not fully understand everything that was happening. He was so young, so innocent. He hadn't even had the chance to experience what it was to be a dragon yet, and to be immortal I was going to have to take that away from him.

My gaze shifted between my son and Black Fang.

"Do not come here and pretend you are brave. Do not be like the others who shunned my wisdom. Do what is needed, and then you will have everything you seek," Black Fang said.

"I'm sorry," I whispered, bowing my head before I did what needed to be done. A sacrifice was necessary. I was ready to do it. I was ready, because after all this time and all this searching, I had finally found the purpose to my life and nothing was going to stop me.

Chapter Twenty Three

K ira
My heart was elated as I returned to the ranch. It felt as though I had just taken my first steps on a new and better path. Once I had made the decision to tell Deke the truth about what he was a load of tension had been lifted from my soul. The only other difficulty was going to be in dealing with Tristan, but that was going to sort itself out one way or another. I looked to Gordy and felt a surge of emotion as I did so. My body was still warm because of him, because of what he had shared in the lake. His kisses had left a mark on me and warm arousal simmered underneath my flesh. It was a fire that had flared into life, one that I had ignored for far too long and would try to never ignore again. There was still a part of me that thought he was too noble for me to deserve, but I had to fight against the part of me that wanted to sabotage things.

I caressed his hand and kissed him before I entered the ranch.

"Come upstairs. I don't want the night to end just yet. There's still a lot we have to talk about and, well, I've been alone for five years. There are a few things I want to catch up on," I said with a playful smile. We crept up quietly, and it made me think about the times I used to sneak out when Dad was sleeping, more often than not to be with Tristan. It was a little confusing how often I kept thinking of Tristan. I wondered if I had actually loved him, or if I had just been attracted to the thrill of being with him.

I nudged Gordy towards my room while I went to check on Deke. I pushed the door open and peeked inside, only for my face to fall away in shock as I saw an empty bed. I cursed. Gordy came rushing up to me and he saw the same thing I did.

"Tristan," I muttered under my breath. Gordy and I ran back downstairs. I didn't even bother to wake my father because time was of the essence. I had no idea where Tristan had taken my son and I felt stupid for leaving Deke alone. I should have known better. I kept repeating this over and over again. Gordy tried to reassure me, but he couldn't understand the shame of seeing your child being put in danger all because of something you had done. We jumped in his truck and raced to Tristan's place, bursting in through the door.

There were no lights on, which puzzled me. I called out for Deke and Tristan, but there was no answer.

"He's not here," Gordy said.

"Then where the hell is he?" I yelled, my eyes blazing with anger. I stormed into every room on the lower floor and was about to march up the stairs when Gordy got my attention.

"I think he's here," he said. He was standing next to a table that had a huge map of the region stretched out alongside it. Tristan had marked the map all over with various notes. There were some circles that had huge crosses in them, but one circle had a big exclamation mark. "He wants Deke to learn about being a dragon, right? Well, what could be better than taking him on a quest to find the oldest dragon there is?"

I stared at the map, fear curdling in my stomach. The world lurched and nausea took hold of me. It was that horrible feeling when you knew that something was deathly wrong yet you weren't sure there was anything you could do about it. I trembled all over with fear as I traced the position of the mountain and then walked out of the ranch, taking flight as soon as I felt the outside air upon my skin. I soared above the clouds and flew as swiftly as I could. Gordy was in hot pursuit of me as well. I scanned the area as we flew, for I did not know how much of a head start Tristan had on me. But he had taken my son and if Deke was in danger there would be hell to pay.

I WAS BREATHLESS AS I reached the mountain and landed, shifting back into my human form. Gordy was behind me, and landed not long after I did. I brushed errant strands of hair away from my face and caught my breath, before looking into the yawning abyss of the cave that led into the mountain.

"Is this it?" Gordy asked.

"I think so. They must have gone inside," I replied. "You know you don't have to be here," I added, wanting to give him a way out.

"I do," he said, smiling at me and squeezing my hand. I have to admit that it felt good to have someone standing by my side. "What if he's really found Black Fang?"

"I don't care what he's found or what he's doing. I'm not going to let anything hurt Deke," I said. We walked into the mountain and there was barely a sliver of light to guide us. We had left in such a hurry that neither of us had thought to bring a flashlight or anything, and I wasn't about to wait for Gordy to rush back to the ranch and get one. But the innards of the mountain were big enough for us to shift into our dragon forms and fly through them. With our heightened senses and improved vision there was no difficulty in making our way through the mountains. If Black Fang was here then it would have to be big enough for him to fly through. I couldn't quite believe that Black Fang was actually real. Would I owe Tristan an apology if it turned out that Black Fang was alive?

Gordy and I flew across a chasm and through a cave filled with spiky pillars that jutted out from the ground and ceiling. There was a grim, foreboding sense as we grew closer to the center of the mountain. I had no idea what we were going to find, and I wasn't entirely sure what Tristan was capable of. He had already tried to get Deke to embrace the dragon inside him by pushing Deke off a cliff. What other lengths would he go to in order to try and get Deke to learn about his true nature? All I wanted was for my son to be safe. If anything happened to him I would never forgive myself.

Then we heard a grim voice. It was so malevolent it sent a shiver down my soul. The way the words sounded... it was as though claws were scraping along the inside of my skull. We emerged just as Black Fang was telling Tristan to sacrifice his son. The cavern was bathed in soft light from some crystals that were embedded into the rock.

"No!" I screamed as I shifted back into human form.

"Mommy!" Deke yelled.

"Intruders!" Black Fang bellowed, the huge behemoth cut an imposing figure in his cavern. Tristan was beside Deke and looked shocked. As soon as Gordy saw Tristan he barreled forth. There was a look of shock and horror on Tristan as Gordy, still in his dragon form, came crashing down and tackled Tristan away.

Black Fang just laughed, a terrifying sound that froze my blood. "Yes... chaos. Fight! Show me who the strongest is, or perhaps I will just take the child for myself. I do thirst for new blood."

"Stay away from my son!" I yelled, not caring that he was around three times my size, not caring that he was the biggest bastard of a dragon I had ever seen, not caring that he was a legend come to life. All I cared about was Deke.

"Do not dare to dictate terms to me," Black Fang snarled. He rose up and leaped towards me, hanging in the air, ready to bring down a terrible claw to strike me. Gordy had seen this though and had left Tristan behind, ready to come and defend me. He thrust himself into Black Fang's flank, using himself as a missile. It barely affected Black Fang though, who turned and swiped a clawed hand towards Gordy, knocking him spinning away.

Tristan used the opportunity to fly back to Deke. "We have to get Deke out of here! He's gone mad."

"MAD?!" Black Fang bellowed and sneered, his golden eyes alive with insane anger, his black scales as foreboding as death itself. "I am the only sane dragon there has EVER been. You are just like the others. You offer yourself to me and then you fail to do what must be done.

You fail to make the sacrifice. There are no dragons as strong as Black Fang. None of you are worthy to be in my presence. Begone!" he yelled, and then opened his violent maw and breathed his fire. It was a sickly green flame, alive with violence and death, ancient and crackling like his soul. I managed to tumble out of its stream as the fire burst against implacable stone. The air was seared with heat. Black Fang snarled with anger. I glanced towards Gordy and Tristan. There was nothing I wanted more than to save Deke, but Tristan was in a better position.

"Tristan, get Deke out of here!" I said, hating that I had to entrust Deke's safety to the man who had put him in danger in the first place, but I had no other choice. Meanwhile I shifted into my dragon form, hoping that I could buy Tristan and Deke some time. I flew into Black Fang's eyeline and breathed fire myself, summoning all my anger and rage and letting it fly in a thrumming stream of amber. It slashed against Black Fang's flank, but I may as well have tried to set the rocks on fire for all the good it did. Black Fang was unaffected and threw his head back, laughing and goading us.

"You are not the first to come to my lair and try to end me. Haven't you learned by now? I am IMMORTAL! There is nothing you can do to tear me from this world. I had hoped you dragons would get wiser over the years, but you are always so pathetic. I am the only one who has seen the light. I am the only one who has heeded the call. It's time I should end you all. NONE of you are fit to share the skies with me," he said, and let another violent burst of fire shoot from his mouth. I spun away, again narrowly avoiding it. Black Fang's huge bulky body began to lift and he moved towards the opening of the mountain. If he got free he wouldn't just kill us and my son, but the whole village too. Everyone's life was at stake. I darted out in front of him and Gordy joined me. We flew in front of Black Fang, dodging his fire as we did so. As we flew through the caverns we craned our necks and shot fire at the stalactites hanging from the cavern ceiling. They wobbled and broke free, falling like daggers onto the dragon that was chasing us.

Some of them splintered as they hit Black Fang's tough hide. Others did hit, but they must have only been pin pricks to him. It was going to take something bigger to take Black Fang down, if it was even possible at all. I looked at Gordy and shared a worried glance with him. We raced through the mountain and broke free, waiting for Black Fang to emerge after us. When he did, Gordy and I both let fly a stream of fire, hoping to scorch his scales and at least have some impact, but he shrugged off the attack as though we had done nothing except breath air on him.

Gordy then flew forward and began hacking away at Black Fang with his claws, trying to pull away the scales and expose a vulnerability. Black Fang twisted around as he attempted to get Gordy off him. His tail flicked in the air. I joined the attack, trying to help Gordy. I could feel something getting loose, but I was so focused on trying to rip the scale from Black Fang's body that I didn't take heed of what he was flying towards. Suddenly I felt a crushing impact as a shadow rushed towards us, only to realize it wasn't a shadow at all, but the hard wall of a mountain. My bones shuddered at the impact and I fell, my wings limp and weak as pain burned through my body. I watched helplessly as Black Fang flew away, flying at great speeds thanks to his huge, expansive wings.

I watched with horror, trying to summon my strength and my willpower. Everything inside me was faltering though and I just wasn't strong enough. Tristan was in the distance, cradling Deke in his arms, but Black Fang bore down on him. I watched with horror. Everything slowed to a crawl as Black Fang opened his maw again and another jolt of fire emerged. There was a burst of smoke and flame and I yelped as I watched it hit Tristan and my son. They spiraled away, his wings simmering with smoke. I roared with anger and flapped my wings, steadying myself as I pushed the pain away and narrowed my gaze onto Black Fang, who was already moving off. I wasn't about to let him get away that easily. I had no idea if Tristan and Deke were still alive, but

I was ready to give my life to avenge them. Black Fang was an evil that had been awakened and I would do everything I could to put him to sleep again.

Chapter Twenty Four

G ordy

Every inch of my body cried out in pain. My heart hurt for Deke, and it burned with anger for Tristan. I had just seen him fall from the sky, falling victim to Black Fang's flames. I had no idea about the state of the boy because I saw Kira fly off in pursuit of Black Fang.

In truth, I was still coming to terms with the fact that I was actually seeing Black Fang in the flesh. For so long I had thought that he was nothing but a story and Tristan was deluded, but Tristan had indeed found him, and what a terrible thing it had been. I wanted to wring Tristan's neck, but it wasn't time for that yet. Black Fang was going to scorch the world if we let him. I grimaced in pain as I followed Kira. She was always quicker than me though, and was already well on the way to catching up with Black Fang. There was no way she could defeat him by herself. I didn't even think we could do it together. He was too big, too tough, had lived too many years to be brought down by two regular dragons. Our fiery breath did nothing, and it would have taken too long to tear away all the scales of his body.

But that didn't mean we couldn't try. I watched her, feeling my heart swell with pride and love as she darted around Black Fang, trying to twist him around and around until he became disoriented. He was a massive creature, but what he had in strength he lacked in agility, and this was Kira's greatest ability. She smoothly flew around him and he was always half a second too slow for her, his claws tearing at empty air, his fiery breath burning away into nothingness. I could sense he was getting frustrated and he was focusing more on Kira than where she was flying. I felt a twitch of anticipation as I saw her heading towards Spear Mountain, which was probably the area we knew the best as we had raced there so many times. I flew there to help her as quickly as I could, hoping that I wouldn't be too late. I wasn't sure what I would have done if I had lost her after we had just begun our journey.

I watched as they flew around Spear Mountain in a spiral, rising higher and higher towards the peak. Black Fang was so big that his body was almost able to wrap around the high, thinner peak completely and I could see that Kira was taking him closer and closer. As I approached I was almost hit by falling debris. Black Fang's scales were cutting against the rock. I dodged the falling stones and I could see what she was trying to do, but it only seemed like a matter of time before Black Fang caught her. He was inexorable and we had been through so much already. I wasn't sure how long her strength would hold out. I pushed myself to my limits, straining until I felt blood trickling out of my nose to ascend to the top with her as well. I watched Black Fang attempt to attack her again. This time his claw almost hit her.

My eyes bulged with desperation. It had taken so much time and so much energy to finally reveal my feelings for her. We were on the cusp of beginning something wonderful and now Black Fang was trying to take it from me. He was trying to take everything. I couldn't let him. I had never been the strongest dragon or the swiftest, but with Tristan knocked out and Kira reaching the limits of her body I was the last one left. Black Fang was getting closer and closer to her with every passing moment and there was only so long she could evade his blows. If he got his claws into her then he would rip her in two, and I was not about to lose her. I opened my jaws wide and let fly a hot jet of fire. I could feel it burning my throat as it came crashing out of me in an orange torrent. The flames did little against Black Fang's tough hide, but it did do enough to distract him from attacking Kira. The brief interlude was enough for Kira to twist around the mountain again. Black Fang's body looked huge against Spear Mountain. He was curled around it like a snake, and I knew I had to try and make this attack count.

Before the flames had had a chance to dissipate I careened towards him, not caring for anything other than the fact that I needed to protect Kira. I opened my mouth and bared my claws and dug them into Black Fang's body. I felt his brittle scales crack under the impact of my teeth and I could feel him tremble in pain. I wondered how long it had been since Black Fang had felt pain. My attack made him crash into Spear Mountain and the great rock trembled. Kira's movements had made him scrape against the side of the mountain all the way up, weakening the foundations, and now as we charged against him we continued to push Black Fang against the mountain. To try and break free of us he writhed and flailed his wings and limbs, roaring as he arched his head back and let out a stream of eldritch fire, which burst harmlessly into the air.

I strained with everything I had. I could tell Kira was too. If it took everything from us then so be it. Black Fang had to die.

We pushed and pressed and the rocks cracked under the bulk of Black Fang. I could feel the world wanting to splinter in two and then it happened. There was a mighty groan as the tip of Spear Mountain toppled and fell. Debris rained down on us and I whimpered in pain as it cut gashes along my skin. I saw Kira being battered by it as well, but there was a hell of a lot more of Black Fang to hit. No matter how he twisted and writhed he was beaten and bruised by the cascading rocks, which sent him plummeting to the ground. He tried to break free. He tried to fly, but the rocks were incessant and then the tip of Spear Mountain fell like a tree, the point of it crashing into his chest. Kira and I dived into the maelstrom of the avalanche and gripped this with our claws, ignoring the scathing touch of jagged rocks as they tore apart our flesh. We pressed it into Black Fang as he pushed back. The tip of the rock was lodged in his chest. He too gripped it with his terrible claws and his head twisted from side to side as he tried to wrench himself free. The air was made hot with fire as he tried to burn us, but the rocks protected us.

Then suddenly it all stopped with a huge crash. There was a sickening crack as the momentum of gravity halted us and the peak of Spear Mountain slid through Black Fang's body, doing lethal damage. His head lolled to the side, his wings were spread out like a blanket across the world, and dark blood trickled from his mouth. There was no movement from his body. Kira and I glanced at each other, wearied and bloodied ourselves, and we quickly flew away from him, watching as the rest of the debris rained down upon the monster, entombing him.

The immortal dragon had just been killed. The legend had been vanquished.

I turned to Kira. There was still no time to waste. She turned and I followed, flying towards Tristan and Deke.

We found them on the ground. My heart had been in my throat as I had thought the worst after seeing Black Fang's flames surround Tristan and Deke. As much as Tristan had angered me, he was still my oldest friend and I did not want to see him dead. Kira landed first and shifted into her human form, running towards them. Tristan was still a dragon. His wings were charred and his body smoldered with heat, but he was moving. Underneath his wing a small figure ran out, crying for his mother. Deke's cheeks were smudged, but otherwise he had been unharmed.

It was a miracle they had survived at all.

Tristan turned to us and everything he needed to say was in his face. His eyes were filled with regret. They glistened with sadness and he wasn't about to stay. He ascended into the air and spread his wings, although his movements were more erratic than usual in his weakened state. He disappeared into the night, and although I had mixed feelings towards him, I still admired him for putting himself in harm's way. It must have hurt so much, but in the end he had protected his child.

Perhaps there was still a chance for him yet.

I shifted back into my human form as well and felt a little awkward as I saw Kira cradling Deke. It seemed to be a moment that I should not have interrupted, but she beckoned me over anyway and wrapped her arm around me.

"That was intense," she whispered. I could feel her trembling. I leaned down to kiss her, knowing how close we had come to death. Deke had his eyes closed as he gripped his mother tightly. I placed my hand on the boy's shoulder, wanting to reassure him that he was safe now and that nothing like this was ever going to happen again. There was a smoky, ashy smell when I placed my head against Kira's and breathed in her fragrance, but I was filled with a deep love. This is where I wanted to be, creating a family with her. I held her close and kissed her forehead, hoping that she would still want to stay even after all this. But for now we had to return home and heal.

We changed into dragons again. It seemed pointless to try and hide the truth from Deke now. Kira carried him away as we flew back to the ranch, tired and drained from the battle, and there was still much left to think about.

Chapter Twenty Five

Tristan

Black Fang was dead.

Black Fang had been a lie.

How had I become so deluded?

Of course there was a reason why the ancient dragons shunned him. I should have known that from the start, but I had been blinded. In that terrible moment when he had asked me to sacrifice my son I saw Black Fang for what he truly was; a monster. There was no way I was going to sacrifice Deke, my own flesh and blood. What was the point of immortal life if it cost the blood of a son I wanted to spend that life with? I had suffered the wounds for it, but that still did not seem like adequate penance.

I retreated from him, knowing that I had sealed my fate and I would never get to see him again. I had let him down as a father and as a dragon. I had betrayed the very essence of my soul and I saw now why Kira had left me in the first place and why she was still so angry with me. I now sat in my dark ranch, shrouded in the shadows of darkness. I huddled on the floor with my knees pulled into my chest and my head bowed, my soul shaking with shame and filled with a lingering feeling that I should have died. The days were going to be long. I thought that perhaps I should be like Black Fang as well and exile myself to ensure that I never darkened the doorstep of the dragons again.

To my surprise there was a knock at the door. I wasn't about to answer it though. I didn't want to see anyone. It opened anyway. Kira stood there, her gorgeous figure a silhouette standing in the doorway. She stepped inside and shook her head.

"It stinks in here," she said. She pulled aside the curtains and bright sunlight filled the room. "Tristan, what the hell are you doing in here?" she asked.

"I'm sorry," I croaked. It was all I could muster, although I knew even if I said it a thousand times it would still not make up for all the trouble I had caused. "I'm so sorry, Kira. I never thought..."

"Your problem wasn't that you didn't think, it was that you didn't listen," she said as she perched herself on the couch. I bowed my head, turning my gaze away from her because I did not deserve to look at her.

"I have so many problems," I said. "All I can say is that I'm sorry. I understand now why you felt the way you do. I have decided that I'm going to leave. I'm going to fly away and live out the rest of my days in the mountains, just as Black Fang did. It's not as much as I deserve, but it shall do. I don't deserve to live among my people. You do, Kira. I know that part of the reason you have been reluctant to stay is because of me, so I want to assure you that I will not be a problem. Let Deke grow up among his own kind. Let him learn what it truly means to be a dragon, the noble kind, not the kind like me." My voice sounded wretched. My soul felt tired. What I really wanted was for her to be angry with me. I wanted her to rant and rave and destroy my ranch after what I had done.

Instead she seemed oddly calm.

"That's a shame, Tristan, because I'm not sure I agree," she said.

I looked up at her with surprise in my eyes. "Aren't you angry?"

"Of course I am. But I'm not just angry at you. I'm angry at myself too. There's no way you should have taken Deke like that, but then again maybe you felt as though you didn't have a choice. It's not as though I gave you a chance to be a father. I just assumed the worst of you, and I'm sorry for that. When the time came, you reminded me of the person I fell in love with all those years ago. When you turned on Black Fang like that, when you turned your back on everything you believed... that's the Tristan I remember. And when you saved my son," she paused for a moment, choking on the emotion in her voice. "Protecting him like that could have killed you. I can't imagine how much it must have hurt, but you did it anyway. You saved my son's life... our son's life, so thank you for that."

"It was the least I could do. I should never have put him in that situation. I should never have taken him to Black Fang."

"You probably shouldn't have," she said, and I thought it was time for the anger to show itself, but it never did. "But the truth is I think being around you has done Deke some good."

"It has?" I asked.

Kira nodded. "Yeah, he's always been a quiet kid and I thought that was just because he didn't have a father, but since he's been back here and since he's been spending time with you I'm starting to see that it's something more. The truth is that I was angry at you for putting him in danger, but when I take a step back I know that I've put him in danger as well, just danger of a different kind. I never knew he was having these dreams. I managed to ignore the dragon part of me, but I should never have prevented him from learning who he was. I think he's been struggling with knowing there's something inside him and being unable to speak about it or understand it. I should have guided him better, like you did. You taught him what he needed to know. You showed him who we are and it's something he needed to see."

"It is?"

Kira nodded again. "Since we came back he hasn't been able to stop talking about it. I thought he might be afraid of it all, but he's not. He's interested. It's his instinct kicking in. It is who he is, after all. It's who he's supposed to be and I've been keeping that from him. I think we've both made mistakes and I just wanted to say that I'm sorry for being an obstacle in your relationship with him. You're right, you are his father and you deserve a chance to be his parent."

"No, I don't. I forced you to leave before. Now I put him in danger. If he stays around me it's only going to be bad for him. He's better off without me."

"I don't think he feels that way," Kira said. "In fact, I brought him with me today because he misses you." She turned and called towards the open door of the ranch. I looked up and my heart melted when I saw a scruffy head peek around the corner. Deke walked in, gazing with wide open eyes at this new place. When he saw me he ran to me and flung his arms around me, as though there was nothing for him to be angry about at all. I felt his warmth and the tight grip of his little arms around me, and it was enough to ground me to the world. My heart swelled and warm tears lined my eyes. I thought that I might end up dying of happiness then and there, because nothing could have been sweeter than feeling the unconditional love of my son. Despite everything I had put him through he was still willing to be near me. There was no sense of fear in his eyes, no sense of hesitation.

"What was it you wanted to tell him, Deke?" Kira asked, nudging their son a little.

Deke rolled his lower lip into his mouth and had a slightly uncertain look in his eyes. "I wanted to ask if you would teach me to fly," he said.

I glanced at Kira, who gave me an encouraging smile. "I'd love to," I replied, feeling a wide smile break out upon my face. Deke clapped his hands together and gave me another quick hug before Kira told him to go and wait outside. Deke's footsteps faded into the distance as Kira turned to look at me.

"I've been thinking about the future a lot lately and I'm going to stick around here. I think it's the best thing for Deke, and I think it's the best thing for me too. I also think it might be good for you. But you're going to have to pull yourself together, Tristan. I don't like you being this crazed recluse who is obsessed with ancient legends. Where's the man I fell in love with? Where's the man who used to race me to the ends of the earth and back again?" she asked. There was a slanted smile on her face as she looked directly into my eyes, and I thought it was just about time to be honest with her.

"I think he went away when you left," I said. The smile faded. I could tell she hadn't been prepared for that answer. "The truth is that I knew I had made a mistake when you went away. It was like a piece of me was missing. I tried to fill it with this search for Black Fang. I thought that if the legend was true and I could find a way to make all the dragons immortal then it would justify the heartache I had been through. I kept telling myself everything requires a sacrifice, and you were the sacrifice I had to pay. I was right as well, because Black Fang wanted me to sacrifice Deke. I want you to know that I never would have done that. It was far easier for me to sacrifice the dreams I had of never dying."

"There's no sense in being immortal if you never truly live. Do you honestly think Black Fang was happy out there? He lived in that dark cavern spending all his days alone. Don't you think it's better to be mortal and at least have a life you can enjoy?"

"It is, and I've learned that lesson, although it took me longer than I would have liked. I don't know what's going to happen in the future, Kira, but I want you to know that I've missed you. I've missed you every day and I wish I had found a better way to tell you this. I haven't been able to stop thinking about the time we spent together and I know we can never get that back. I know there's something between you and Gordy, but I-" my words were cut short as I felt her lips pressing against mine. They were soft and sweet, and all the swirling sensations that used to whirl around me came alive again, having lain dormant for all these years. Her hand wrapped around the nape of my neck and her fingers ran through my hair. When she leaned back I looked at her, confused.

"Like I said, I've been doing a lot of thinking. That was a thank you for what you did for Deke. But it was also... I kind of wanted to see if something was still there," she giggled with girlish glee as she said this.

"And is it?" I asked. Kira answered me by kissing me again. I wasn't entirely sure what this meant, but I definitely wanted to find out. She pressed her forehead against me and spoke in a breathy voice.

"I'm finally home," she said. "After I've been getting so angry with you I realized it was because I think there's something still between us, some unfinished business. You've been lost for a long time, Tristan. When I left I was furious because I thought you should have come looking for me, but now I'm wondering if it was actually the other way around."

"But what about Gordy?"

"I do feel strongly for him as well," she said as her brow furrowed. "I'm not willing to betray him after he's been so kind for me I just... I can't sort out these feelings by choosing only one of you. I know it's going to be difficult, and I guess you're going to have to talk to each other about it, but I think I'd like to try exploring things with both of you."

I was surprised at this turn of events, but not unhappy about it.

"And what about Deke? Won't he find the whole thing confusing?"

"Maybe... but if he can get used to being a dragon then I think he can get used to this as well. It's not as though his life is ever going to be conventional. Just... just think about it, okay?" she said, patting me on the chest. She kissed me again and when she did I knew that I would never be able to resist her.

However, I wasn't sure how Gordy was going to feel about things.

I SPOKE TO HIM SHORTLY after Kira left. I found him by his ranch, working on his truck. There was a wary look in his eyes as I approached. He nodded towards me.

"I want to say I'm sorry, Gordy, for everything. You've always been such a good friend to me and I repaid you by being a bastard. I should have listened to you when you told me that I was going too far. I hope that we can go back to being friends again, eventually. I thought it was really impressive, the way you dealt with Black Fang."

"Thanks," Gordy said, not giving anything away.

"I just spoke with Kira. She told me how she feels about things and what she wants after she stays here. I just... I wondered how you feel about it all?" I asked.

Gordy raised his eyebrows and sighed, before running a hand along his jaw. "I can't say it's how I pictured things working out, but I can't get angry for her wanting what she wants. Besides, when I think about it, it's always been the three of us, hasn't it?"

"It has. Maybe things would be different now if you had been involved more in the past," I admitted.

"Look, I'm not sure how it's going to work and I don't know if we're going to drive each other crazy, all I know is that I want the best for Kira and if this makes her happy then so be it. If you're going to be the man you used to be then that's fine too, but if you ever get an idea like this in your head again, or you start going crazy and push her away again, I will make sure you end up like Black Fang," he said through gritted teeth. He bristled with power and it was a side of him he rarely showed. I could see why Kira was drawn to him. I nodded, and extended my hand.

"Let's agree that we're going to do what's best for Kira then, and Deke," I said. Gordy stared at my hand for what seemed an interminable length of time, before he finally clasped it. I looked into the eyes of my good friend. I had trusted him with so many things over the years, so there wasn't really any difficulty in trusting him with the woman I loved either.

I had gone from being hated among my own kind to suddenly being accepted again. It was going to take some getting used to, but it was certainly better than the alternative. I glanced towards the mountains as I left Gordy, grateful that I wasn't going to have to make them my home just yet.

Chapter Twenty Six

K ira
My heart was still in turmoil. There were moments when I thought I was crazy for feeling the way I felt, but I couldn't help it. There was still something between Tristan and I no matter how many times I tried to deny it, and in the end I just couldn't keep fighting it any longer. I hated putting Gordy through this, but he seemed to be open to it. I spent time with each of them alone at first. There was a little anxiety when I allowed Tristan to look after Deke, but Deke came home each time bursting with excitement and eager to tell me what he had learned. The more time I spent with Tristan the more I saw the man I had fallen in love with when I was younger. He still had that unerring ability to make me laugh and make me think anything was possible. With Gordy it was different. Calmer. I could not choose between the two men and I know that it may seem greedy of me to want to enter into a relationship with both of them at the same time, but I had spent five years denying my true nature and shunning love completely, so I felt that I was due a little leeway in this regard.

There were many long conversations about how this was going to work. It was only going to be viable if we were all open with each other, especially when we were struggling with things. I think the fact that we had been friends before helped us in this regard. It had taken a bit of time for Gordy to forgive Tristan for the way he acted, but they had been spending more time together too and were acting more like I was used to them acting. It helped Deke to be surrounded by so many people who enjoyed his company as well. He came alive in a way he never had before in the city, and I was filled with guilt for keeping him away from his home for such a long time. I could only hope that when he grew up he would forgive me for that. He was never fazed by anything he learned, or by seeing us turning into dragons. He was still yet to shift, but he was learning more every day.

I have to say that finally being open with him about our true ancestry brought us closer together as well. I had never fully realized just how much tension I had held in my body regarding this, and how much I had been hiding from him. Being home had brought me closer to my own son, and that was something I would always be thankful for.

But there was one aspect of my relationship with Gordy and Tristan that I was eager to try. My desire for them both spiraled through me as though ribbons were flying, and while I enjoyed making love to them both individually, I wanted to try it with them both at the same time. So one evening I left Deke in the care of Rock and we went over to Tristan's place. We drank and laughed and reached the point where we slurred our words. I placed the bottle in the middle of the room and then sauntered over to Gordy, kissing him passionately. I figured that it was better to show them what I intended than merely talking to them about it. When I was done with Gordy I did the same thing to Tristan, and then stood in between them. They were still sitting on the floor, looking up at me as though I was a goddess.

"There's been something on my mind, boys," I said coyly, "something I want to try. It's another little adventure for us to go on. Are you game?" I asked, the words dripping from my mouth like nectar. I raised my arms as I spoke and spun around slowly, showing off the pleasing curves of my body. They were entranced and neither of them resisted. They were drawn to me like moths to a flame and within moments they were standing beside me, the air around me being scorched with the passionate heat that bristled from their bodies.

Both men were wearing plaid shirt and jeans. Their sleeves were rolled up their forearms, showing the tanned skin and hinting at the muscles beyond. Tristan was a few inches taller than Gordy, while Gordy was a little stockier. I was smaller than each of them, tilting my neck back to look at them properly. I placed a hand on each of their chests as their hands slipped around my back, making me feel so petite. I wore a simple vest top and the left strap kept slipping down my shoulder, almost as though it was aching to be free. With every breath my chest rose, heaving with passion. My lips parted as I felt us slipping into this other world, this world filled with passion and desire and lust. The air crackled with all these things and more, and as their lips kissed my neck my body melted into them, only continuing to be suspended in the air because my arms were draped around their shoulders.

In one swift, sudden movement they lifted me off my feet and I was filled with exhilaration. I laughed as they carried me to the bedroom and threw me onto the heavy bed. The mattress creaked under the impact. The sheets were soft against my skin. I got to my knees as they stood at the end of the bed, standing shoulder to shoulder, both men in their prime, both men radiating power and masculinity. A dark desire stirred within me and flowed throughout my body, making me feel more and more alive with every moment that passed. I had spent so long denying myself so many things, and now it was time for me to make up for those hollow times.

I reached out and began unbuttoning their shirts. One by one the buttons fell away, the fabric opening up like curtains on a theater stage, ready to see a display of taut flesh and sculpted muscles. I groaned as I ran my hands through the bed of chest hair that ran along their exposed flesh, following it down as it narrowed to a thin line, ending at the denim. The belts clinked as I worked them with my hands, feeling satisfaction as the buckles were undone. The men ran their hands behind my head and leaned down, stealing kisses from me. Some of them were soft. Some of them were hard. All of them were fucking amazing and sent tingles shooting all the way down my body, right to the tips of my toes.

I shuddered and laughed with glee, completely overwhelmed by the intense sensations that were flowing through me. The belts came away. I fumbled with the rest of their jeans, but by this point my hands were trembling too much to make any difference. Gordy and Tristan did it themselves and I watched as the jeans were pulled away, inch by inch revealing themselves. My lips parted as I saw their aroused erections stretching the fabric of their underwear. I reached out immediately, feeling something twitch in the molten core of me as I pulled the fabric away, needing to get to their flesh as though I was drowning and this was the only source of air.

I took a deep gulp as my gaze danced upon their taut flesh. The smooth tips stared at me, the rivers of veins rippled with strength and the hair at the base of the shaft framed it in manliness. The smell of their sex burned the air and I breathed it in gladly, wanting to gorge myself on them. I had one hand for each of them. Despite their differences, Gordy and Tristan looked like reflections of each other. My slender fingers curled around their shafts. The heat burned my palms, but it was such a wonderful sensation. My heart trembled and I could feel pinpricks of heat dancing upon my body as a tight knot unwound inside me. I brought my hands back and forth, stroking them, watching the pleasure dance upon their faces. Their muscles were tight, their bodies perfect, and I knew that making love with two of them was going to be far more intense than making love with each of them individually.

I leaned forward, my hair falling across my face as I opened my mouth, wondering which of them I was going to taste first. But then a strong hand pulled my neck back, flinging me to the bed. I lost grip of their erections and I stretched my arms in the hope of reaching them again.

"It's not fair for us to be naked while you're still dressed," Tristan said with a cocky arch of his eyebrow. I smiled as they descended upon me. Gordy pulled off my top, ripping it away without any difficulty at all. He then reached around and unclasped my bra, tossing it away to join the puddle of clothes that had formed on the floor. My breasts poured out, and Gordy's hands were quick to fondle them. I gasped, the breath sharp and jagged in my throat. My nipples hardened immediately as his fingers drifted across the rising curves of my breasts. The sensitive skin sent waves of heat pulsing through me, which reverberated around my body and made me feel as though I was going to explode.

Meanwhile, Tristan was pulling away my skirt. As soon as it was gone he took my panties and dragged them down, wasting no time in exposing my sweet, aching pussy. He clamped his hands on my thighs and pinned my legs apart, gazing at me with hunger. While Gordy was still playing with my breasts I felt Tristan's breath sweeping against my thighs, and then suddenly his tongue was playing with me. My head arched back and my mouth opened. A low, guttural moan burst out of me as I felt his tongue twisting against my most sensitive area, but it was suffocated as Gordy kissed me. The men held me like this, Gordy kissing me and playing with my breasts, while Tristan buried himself in me.

Gordy leaned back and allowed me to watch Tristan's head locked in between my thighs. The pleasure curled inside me and came thrumming through me like lightning bolts. I shuddered and moaned and I reached out to grab onto anything. My left hand found the sheets of the bed and I clutched them in a tight fist. My other hand found Gordy's erection. I clung to the hot flesh and started working it again, stroking and massaging it, loving the tense murmurs that erupted from Gordy's soul. The air was alive with our passion and a dreamy haze settled over my mind, for I was unable to concentrate properly as Tristan was making a mess of me.

Gordy took my head and twisted me around. Finally I could taste him. I closed my eyes as I felt him slide into my mouth, so hard, so fiery, hitting the back of my throat with his desire. Saliva dribbled out of the corners of my mouth. I wanted to scream because of what Tristan was doing to me, but Gordy had me choking on him.

When he allowed me to catch my breath I looked down. Tristan was rising, his lips shining with the sweetness of the streaming passion that had poured from me. He rose up and kissed me. I tasted myself on his lips. It was tangy and sweet and then his palm pressed against me. I don't know what he was doing, but it made this vibrating sensation pass through my entire body and it sent this delirious, exquisite jolt of pleasure shooting through me.

I wanted more.

I needed more.

Fuck he was good.

Gordy kissed me too. I was passed between the two men, all the while Tristan was playing with me. I closed my eyes to enjoy the sensations and then suddenly when I looked up it was Gordy whose fingers were dancing inside me. I had no idea when the men had switched. It was as though a magic trick had been played upon me. My skin was flushed. It burned and pulsed and throbbed. The ecstasy swam through me and grew in intensity, rising like a great wave until it reached a crescendo and I felt like doubling over, as though something had been pulled directly from me.

I shuddered again and if it hadn't have been for the men I would have fallen back to the bed, melting into the sheets without any hope of remaining upright.

But they continued to hold me in their strong arms, they continued to play with me with their endless energy. I clung to them, holding onto their muscles, feeling so weak and vulnerable as they brought me to this delirious place where I was so frail and fragile and could do nothing aside from scream and moan with sheer delight. Pleasure soared within me and I felt as though I was flying again, but this time it was only my soul taking flight rather than everything else. My breath slammed against the air as I exhaled, in between the fervent kisses the men were showing me, and I was beginning to wonder if I had stretched myself beyond my limits.

There were two of them and only one of me, and they weren't going to stop until they were fully satisfied. My thighs were already slick with lust and when they took hold of me I could feel the dampness on their fingers. They turned me around so that I was on my knees. Tristan stood behind me, running a hand along my spine, before grabbing my ass, sinking his fingers into my feminine flesh. Gordy was at my head, spreading his legs around me. One hand guided my mouth to his erection, while the other reached underneath and played with my breasts again. Hot pleasure was coming at me from every angle and I wasn't sure where to feel it first. It just came at me in this tsunami and then they took me at the same time. My lips locked around Gordy's cock at the same time as Tristan thrust into me. Pain blurred with pleasure as I felt both men take me from either side. Stinging tears appeared in my eyes, but this is what I wanted. This is what I needed.

I looked up at Gordy and began sucking as hard as I could while Tristan was behind me, his hips drilling into me, his flesh slapping against mine. I groaned as much as I could while Gordy's cock was in my mouth. Saliva continued to drizzle down. His tip was red, raw and so delicious. Tristan's was thick and long, and it slammed against the deep parts of me that hid inside. He had a strong grip on my body as he fucked me, and I was caught between these two men as a miasma rose in my mind and spread throughout my body, catching me in this wondrous, glorious feeling that was more intense than I had ever felt before.

I yelped in pain as Tristan grabbed a fistful of my hair and pulled me away from Gordy. He twisted me around and pushed me onto my back, coming over me as though he was spreading his wings. He always did like to be rough. He kissed me as the beast inside him took over and his body moved by instinct more than anything else. He rocked and writhed and his hips were like pistons, ready to take me to heaven and then slam me back to earth mercilessly. The sensations careened through my body and I was a mess with my flushed cheeks and strands of my hair matted to my sweat covered scalp. I knew Gordy was still to come as well, and that's what made it almost frightening.

My arms lay splayed to the side of me as Tristan made love to me, crashing and slamming my body relentlessly. My mouth screamed with pleasure. My eyes begged for more and he was willing to oblige. I felt him tremble inside me, then suddenly every muscle in his body went taut as the heat exploded, a torrent of passion that burst in a wave of pleasure and left me gasping. My mind was a kaleidoscopic haze and my body was drained, but that was just one man.

Another was to come.

Tristan was a sweaty mess as he pulled out of me, gasping with deep breaths as he leaned back on his haunches. I had a brief moment to collect myself before I was pulled around again. Tristan gathered my limp body in his arms and turned me around, this time pulling me to my knees and pushing me onto Gordy. He caught me and kissed me breathlessly. The tension in his body was tight. He had been waiting for this. His hands slipped around my waist as I straddled him, shifting my position so that our bodies could become one. I groaned as I felt him enter me. I was so tender and sensitive and in a way I couldn't believe that I could still be feeling this much pleasure, but I was ready to be fucked until I passed out.

In my fervent mania I cupped Gordy's head in my hands and kissed him deeply, rocking back and forth gently to get used to the feeling of him inside me. The orgasmic energy that surged through my body bathed me, and was just one long unending stream that had begun when Tristan had first touched me that night. Mine and Gordy's tongue danced. I could still feel Tristan's presence near us, and this added another electric sensation to the evening. Gordy's hands were tight against my body, his lips were tender though, and I could feel myself falling into him, as though he was an abyss into which I wanted to launch myself.

I rocked my body back and forth, enjoying the terse moans that escaped his mouth, but then something switched inside him. I felt his grip on me tighten. One of his hands reached up to the back of my neck and held me tightly, stopping me from moving. It was his turn to take control. The bed creaked again, so violently I thought it was going to break as he thrust into me, using his strength to slam into my body. The angle was just right to where he seemed to reach my very soul. I groaned, my eyes rolling into the back of my head as I flung my arms around him, holding onto him for what seemed like dear life. The pleasure was a cacophony within me, as though it had taken on life of its own, as though I had been baptized and was embracing this new sensation. It was a veil had been lifted and I was seeing things for the first time.

Then Tristan came beside me and twisted my head towards him, kissing me deeply while Gordy was fucking me. It was the last thing I needed to be taken over the line and it all poured through me, this hot, cloying, molten energy that burned and scorched in such a pleasing way. I crumpled as the pleasure shot through me. Gordy's body was strong and fierce, and it all lashed through me as though I was being whipped from the inside. I lay against him, with Tristan beside me too, feeling complete, feeling as though this was how my life should always have been lived. I was with my two men, my two loves, who completed me in different ways. I had taken myself away from this dragon world for five years, but now that I was back I knew I was never going to leave again because I had everything I had ever wanted right here.

I was finally happy, and I knew that Deke would be happy too.

Chapter Twenty Seven

G ordy

Being in a relationship with Kira and Tristan wasn't something I had always had in mind, but I guess it felt natural and after some growing pains we had found a nice rhythm. With someone else to look after Deke it gave me and Kira a chance to be alone, and I didn't mind looking after Deke either. I had always said that I would do anything to be with Kira, and the truth is that after our experience with Black Fang, Tristan was back to being the man I had known before. It felt as though I had gotten my friend back and I couldn't have been happier.

We fell into a good rhythm, and I was more than glad that Kira wasn't going to return to the city. Her place was with us, and Deke was excited to be able to learn about our history as dragons. Tristan was in his element as he spoke about all the old stories, and Deke listened intently. I have to admit that I did as well, and in a way I rekindled something of my love for being a dragon as well. It was easy to take it for granted having lived with it for a number of years, but when I thought about the rich history and how few of us there were... it really reminded me that we were special.

I had flown out to Black Fang's tomb a few times, just to make sure that the dragon was really dead. The rocks were undisturbed, so I breathed with relief. The last thing we needed was for him to appear again. However, it did mean that Tristan's quest had not been fulfilled, so the dragons were still prone to dying, which wasn't good news for Rock.

Seeing his daughter and his grandson had given his fortitude a boost, but his health faltered after this. It was sad to see such a strong and vigorous man being weathered by illness, his skin becoming looser and sallow, his eyes cloudy, and his breath haggard. He acted like it was no big deal, and seemed to be happy with the life he had lived. It wasn't the same for Kira though. She blamed herself for having missed out on a good chunk of time with her father. No matter how much Rock tried to absolve her of blame she just couldn't seem to accept it, and neither me or Tristan seemed to be able to help.

I guess this was one of the good things about being in a triad relationship. Tristan and I could speak about Kira's state of mind and try and find a way to make things better for her. Sadly, I wasn't sure anything could help apart from time.

The sun shone brightly in an azure sky when Rock finally died. It was a momentous day, actually, because it was the day when Deke embraced the beast inside him for the first time. He had been speaking openly about his dreams and the more he learned about dragons, the more his dreams came into focus. It reached the point where he was able to become the dragon and take control in his dream, which was the last step before taking control in real life.

"I'm so nervous," Kira said.

"You don't have to be nervous. This is what he was born to do," Tristan replied, wearing a proud smile. There were times when I did feel a little left out with things, as Deke was never going to truly be my child. I tried not to let it show though. We were all standing outside, although Rock was sitting in a chair we had brought for him. The poor guy didn't have the strength to stand under the unforgiving heat. Deke was standing on a precipice, holding his arms out just as his father had instructed him to do. It was something we had all been through before. I remember how nervous I had been when it had been my time. All my family were stood behind me in a line, ready to cheer me on. It hadn't helped me though. I felt the pressure of not wanting to disappoint them. I wondered if Deke felt the same thing now. Tristan had been there that day too, and I remember feeling more confident thanks to the fact that my friend was with me.

I chuckled to myself, for I had never known our lives would end up like this.

"Go on, Deke, you can do it, just remember what I taught you. Feel the air. Listen to your instincts. This is who you are meant to be. Set yourself free and fly," Tristan said.

I glanced towards Kira, who had her hands clasped together, something she did when she was nervous. There was no way Deke would have been able to do this if they had stayed in the city and I was glad that she had brought Deke here. It was only right that they should be allowed to be who they truly were. She began clapping her hands, offering encouragement, and I joined in soon after. Even Rock was cheering the boy on. Deke nodded and then stepped forward, taking a drop off the precipice. I knew it was taking Kira everything to not shift into a dragon and hurl herself off the cliff too to ensure that Deke was safe, but there was no need this time. For a moment there was silence, but then movement as a small dragon came flying up. His scales were the same shade as his mother, and he seemed to have her gift for speed as well. His body flicked and darted this way and that.

A smile broke out upon our faces.

"I think he wants a race," Tristan said. He ran forward and then threw himself into the air, shifting into a dragon as he did so. Deke surged off and Tristan was in hot pursuit.

I looked across at Kira. Her eyes glistened with tears.

"I can't believe he's a dragon. I'm so... so proud of him," she said. I wrapped my arm around her and kissed her on the forehead.

"He looks just as majestic as his mother," I said.

"Is that right, Dad?" she asked, turning to Rock. There was no reply though. "Dad?" she asked, moving away from me and reaching out with concern towards her father. She touched his hand and caressed his cheek, but we both knew he had gone. The light of life had dimmed from his eyes and there was no flicker of movement anywhere on his body.

"Dad..." she said weakly, her head bowing with sorrow. I went to her and held her as she wept.

"At least the last thing he saw was the future taking flight," I said in a low voice, hoping that my words would bring her some comfort. "Maybe he was waiting to see Deke do that. He can rest now. He was in so much pain."

"It's not fair, it's just not fair," Kira wailed, pressing her head into the nape of my neck. I held her shuddering body tightly, wishing I could do anything to take the pain away, but I knew that all I could do was be there for her.

WE HAD MANAGED TO TAKE Rock back to his ranch and place him in his bed for the time being. I asked Kira what she wanted to do now, and all she said was that she didn't want to be locked inside.

"I think Dad would have appreciated me taking flight. I need to be out there," she said, gazing towards the sky. I was more than happy to oblige, for I always loved seeing her embrace her dragon form and soar through the sky. We left the ranch behind and shifted, our long, serpent like bodies stretching across the sky. We gracefully flapped our wings and headed towards the mountains, to the deserted land where no human eyes would peer at us. This time, however, we did not race. We flew softly, gently, and were drawn to Spear Mountain.

It looked like its name no longer. The protruding tip had been broken off, and now there was just a jagged, slanted surface that looked like a poorly made table. We flew to it and landed on this surface, gazing out at the world. I stood beside Kira, holding her in my arms.

"I'm so sorry this happened, Kira. If there was anything I could have done to change it..." I said helplessly.

"Be careful what you say there, because you might start down the path Tristan went down," she said with a wry smile. "I think we're going to have to come up with a new name for this mountain. We can hardly call it 'Spear Mountain' when there is no spear."

"Maybe Broken Spear Mountain?" I suggested. It was a weak joke, but it was enough to make her laugh.

"You know, I used to dream about this place when I lived in the city. I hated waking up and remembering it. This place was always calling back to me, and all I wanted to do was forget it."

"You can't forget something that is such an important part of you, Kira. Believe me I wish life was that easy, but it's not."

"It just makes me wonder, you know, about what this place is going to be like when I'm Dad's age. These rocks and mountains and this desert, it never seems to change that much, but we change a lot."

"It changes too, it just takes more time. One thing is for sure, now that you're back there's going to be a better future for us, and I bet Rock knew that too. I think he passed on content in knowing that you will carry on his legacy and teach all your children what they need to know."

"I just feel so bad about leaving him for those five years. If I had known he was going to die now..."

"You might well have left anyway. It was always difficult to get you to change your mind. It still is," I said. This remark brought a smile from her.

"Gordy, I never wanted things to be this difficult. I never wanted things to be this painful. We're going to be okay, aren't we? I hate to think that we're going to have to go through something like this again."

I placed my hands around her shoulders and looked her directly in the eyes. "Kira, we have each other. That's all we need, and if that's not enough we have Tristan too," I said.

Kira's smile flickered on her face. "I haven't forced you into anything, have I? I just hate to think that I'm hurting anyone."

"You're not forcing anyone into anything. I'm with you because I love you. I love Tristan too, even though sometimes he drives me crazy. But there is something I want to talk to you about. You know that I love Deke and we get on great, but there are some moments, like today, when I feel a little bit out of the loop. I respect the fact that you and Tristan are his biological parents and I don't want to get in the way of the bond you have, but it's gotten me thinking that I'd like to experience that bond for myself. I know you probably don't want to think about that yet given how you just lost Rock and you're still coming to terms with being back here, but I wanted to see how you felt about starting a family one day," my gaze drifted away from her as I was afraid of seeing a pitying look in her eyes, the look of someone who couldn't give me what I asked for. However, she responded to my words with a deep kiss, one that ran right to my very heart.

"I think it's a wonderful time for it," Kira said. "In fact, I couldn't think of a better time. Deke is old enough to have a brother or sister, and this time I want to raise my child in the right place. I don't want to ever have to hide who I am again, or to ignore what makes them special. We're dragons, and that should be something that's never hidden," she said.

My heart leaped for joy and I kissed her again, this time grabbing her in my arms with a whole load of passion. I could feel it coursing through my body and I was ready to start trying for a child with her then and there, but two shadows came over us. I looked up and saw the father and son swirling overhead, circling us like vultures. They descended to the mountain and shifted into their human forms. Deke didn't break his stride, running straight into Kira's arms.

"Mommy, Mommy, did you see? I flew so high! Daddy took me all around the mountains and I even beat him! He said that I'm the fastest dragon he's ever seen! Can I go again? Please? Please!" he asked, bouncing up and down with excitement. We were all so happy for him, and I couldn't wait until I had a child of my own to share this moment with him, although it would be some years before I experienced that joy. Knowing it was coming was enough though.

"I think you've had enough excitement for one day. You don't want to wear yourself out. The last thing you want is to get tired while you're high in the air, because then the only way is down," Kira said, sending her fingers plummeting to the surface of the mountain, pretending that her hand was Deke. Deke laughed and sighed, accepting his mother's judgment for now. She ruffled his head and kissed him, pride etched upon her face. "So your Dad thinks you're the fastest dragon, eh? Well, I've been known to be pretty fast too. I think next time you go out flying I'm going to have to come with you and we'll see if you can beat me," Kira said. Deke seemed excited for the challenge.

"It's great to see him so happy, isn't it," Tristan said. He was beaming with pride too, and the look upon his face was far different to the crazed, obsessed one that had plagued me for the past five years. He seemed more relaxed now that he had Deke in his life, and Kira by his side again. Having been with him over the last five years I perhaps hadn't seen how drastic the change had been in him, so I was glad that he had salvaged his sanity.

"It is, and he's going to need to enjoy this moment because it's not always going to last," I replied.

"What do you mean by that?" Tristan asked, furrowing his brow.

I lowered my voice to ensure that Deke would not be able to hear my words. It wasn't my place to tell him the tragic news of his grandfather's death. "Rock died. I think he was waiting to see Deke take flight. He died happily, at least."

Tristan exhaled slowly and his head dropped. "I suppose we all knew it was coming, but it's still a tragedy."

"Don't get any ideas," I warned him, showing a playful look in my eyes as I was trying to lighten the mood. He grinned back.

"I've made that mistake once and I won't be repeating it. Besides, Kira helped me to see sense. Being immortal isn't any good if you don't have people to share your life with. Life is about making the most out of each day you have, not of trying to cheat the system and be alive to see every day, especially not when it costs so much. I'm just glad it didn't take me longer to learn that lesson."

"Me too," I said. "You know, you should be real proud of that kid. He's a great boy."

"I am, and I hope that you can feel the same one day."

"I'm sure I will," I said, and Tristan could tell that something had happened from the look in my eyes. His smile widened and he placed his hand on my shoulder, squeezing me tightly. There were still lots of things to take care of. The oncoming days were going to be hard as Deke was going to have to learn about death. There would be a funeral and emotions would be low and despairing, but through it all there was going to be hope for the future, a future I thought had been beyond me until Kira had returned.

She had breathed new life into me, into us, and our relationship may have been unconventional, but it worked for us. I looked beyond the dark days and thought of the future when she and I would be teaching our child about the history of the dragons, and I was sure that more children would follow still.

We walked over to join Kira and Deke. Tristan and I flanked her, and both of us gazed at her with an adoring look in our eyes. We were a family of dragons and we were where we belonged, with each other. The sun beat down upon us and then Kira dropped to her knees, whispering in Deke's ear, but loud enough so that we could hear.

"I think I was wrong. Maybe there is enough time for another flight," she said. Deke looked excited as he and his Mom jumped off the edge of the mountain, followed by Tristan and I. We flew back home, our wings spread in a glorious display of our power, knowing that nothing could threaten our happiness again.

Enjoy what you read? Please leave a review!

Don't miss out!

Visit the website below and you can sign up to receive emails whenever Lilly Wilder publishes a new book. There's no charge and no obligation.

https://books2read.com/r/B-A-KAQD-DZEYC

BOOKS 2 READ

Connecting independent readers to independent writers.

Did you love *Dragon Lovers*? Then you should read *Wolf's Mate*[1] by Lilly Wilder!

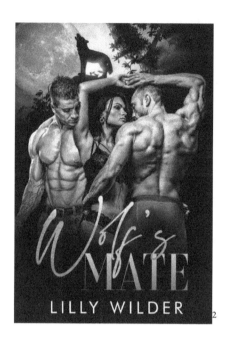

[2]

Desperate And Afraid, I Need To Stay Hidden, So They Offer To Protect Me, But At What Cost? I've always been a good girl, a sheltered girl.

I guess I have my extremely rich dad to thank for that.

I want to escape the reputation that follows our name, but you can never get the stink of money off of you. It's a smell that attracts hungry beasts... just like blood.

The one time I finally decide to let go and live a little, something terrible happens. I find unlikely protectors in the two wolf shifters who save me, but they want something in return. Their clan is in danger of dying out unless they find mates willing to produce offspring.

---

1. https://books2read.com/u/4DnnD7

2. https://books2read.com/u/4DnnD7

They want a good girl to break the rules.

But, can she?

Wolf's Mate is a standalone paranormal romance with a HEA and NO cheating!

Also by Lilly Wilder

Indebted To The Vampires
Wolf's Nanny
Bearly Familiar
Protected by the Wolves
Bear Protection
Dragon Dreams
Seduced by Dragons
Her Lion Protectors
Rescued By The Wolves
Captured By The Dragons
Academy For Vampires
Her Biker Wolves
Bad Boy Dragons
Wild Wolves
Wolf's Mate
Dragon Lovers

Milton Keynes UK
Ingram Content Group UK Ltd.
UKHW010848280324
440101UK00001B/96